TABOR EVANS

LONGARM

SETS THE STAGE

D1561703

JOVE BOOKS, NEW YORK

This is a work of fiction. Names, characters, places, and incidents either are the product of the author's imagination or are used fictitiously, and any resemblance to actual persons living or dead, business establishments, events, or locales is entirely coincidental.

LONGARM SETS THE STAGE

A Jove Book / published by arrangement with
the author

PRINTING HISTORY
Jove edition / September 2004

Copyright © 2004 by Penguin Group (USA) Inc.

For information, address: The Berkley Publishing Group,
a division of Penguin Group (USA) Inc.,
375 Hudson Street, New York, New York 10014.

ISBN: 0-515-13813-4

A JOVE BOOK®
Jove Books are published by The Berkley Publishing Group,
a division of Penguin Group (USA) Inc.,
375 Hudson Street, New York, New York 10014.
JOVE and the "J" design
are trademarks belonging to Penguin Group (USA) Inc.

PRINTED IN THE UNITED STATES OF AMERICA

10 9 8 7 6 5 4 3 2 1

Chapter 1

There was more than one way to skin a cat or separate a sporting gent from his money. Honest John Krebbs favored private poker games by invite only in the honeymoon suite of the Cosmopolitan Hotel.

A younger, leaner and meaner loner known only to himself as the Great Garrick was aiming to leave the game with all the money in his own less friendly way, once he managed to horn in past a locked and guarded door.

This did not figure to be easy. As a man who kept abreast of sporting events in other parts, Honest John was on the prod that night, and so he'd retained the services of the expensive but reliable Trigger Tanner, the former Texas Ranger who said he'd lived through Chicamauga, to man that one hall door and make certain nobody without a damned fine reason barged in on a serious sporting event staged for high rollers and high rollers alone.

So nobody had, since the appointed hour of 8 P.M., save for the five invited suckers, Honest John and his one-man private army posted at the door, and from time to time the room service bellhop, loaded down with yet another tray of refreshments.

He, like everyone else, came and went by Trigger's

leave. The former ranger had suggested the hotel send up trays from the taproom or kitchen only by prearranged signal, with Honest John's approval, as soon as he'd studied on it. Honest John had chosen the Cosmopolitan because it was as high-toned and up-to-date a hotel as one might find in Tombstone, with gas lighting, indoor plumbing and fancy room service bell cords to save guests having to holler down the stairs.

At Honest John's suggestion, along about ten, Trigger pulled the room service cord nearest the hall door. Through the marvels of modern mechanics, a bell chimed and the room number of the honeymoon suite was exposed by a slide-away sheet metal cover. So in due time the bellhop on duty showed up in his brass-buttoned serving livery to take everybody's orders.

Serious high rollers knew better than to dull their minds with red-eye or to make themselves sleepy by overstuffing their guts. So everybody but a recently rich mining man with a lot to learn about poker ordered another round of black coffee and, whilst the kitchen was at it, some whores' ovaries or bitty-ass sandwiches invented in Paris, France. It took about a dozen of the sissy things to feel like a regular sandwich. So they were safe to sort of nibble betwixt hands.

The bellhop left with their orders and most everyone but Trigger had sort of forgot about him by the time he was knocking on the door again. Trigger cracked the door, opened wider at the sight of brass buttons in the dim gaslight and let the squirt most of the way in with his heavy tray before he suddenly whipped out his Schofield .45 to throw down on the startled bellhop and demand, "What's going on here! You ain't our regular bellhop!"

The slender figure holding the heavy tray in both hands replied in as outraged a tone, "Is that any reason to shove a gun in my face, mister? I'd be Chad's relief if it's all

2

the same to you. Can I put this infernal tray down somewheres?"

Trigger pointed with his gun muzzle at a sideboard gainst a far wall as he asked, suspiciously, "It ain't eleven yet, and Chad told me he works as late as midnight."

As he crossed the rug with his tray, the object of the former ranger's suspicions replied in a disgusted tone, "Well, of course Chad's on until midnight, and this is a payday night. I hate to be the one to have to tell you this, mister, but we have other guests in this hotel tonight, and some of them tip better. I'll tell Chad you don't want anybody serving you but him. Now that I see why he asked me to take this call."

He set the tray down and turned as if to go. From across the room Honest John called, "Not so fast, sonny. Bring that tray over here and serve all these gents without they have to leave the table."

Trigger volunteered, "I'll handle that, boss. Soon as I send this fresh mouth with a strange face on its merry way!"

Honest John snorted, "Never hired you as a serving wench, no offense. He ain't that strange to me. Seen him around the lobby downstairs earlier."

So Trigger shut and barred the hall door as the vaguely familiar bellhop brought the serving tray over to the table.

Later police reports would argue some about the exact time gunfire was heard from somewhere up above by staff and guests not directly involved in the massacre. It was generally agreed there'd been a fusillade of a dozen or more pistol shots interspersed with what had sounded like a double-barreled bird gun, mayhaps a sixteen-gauge. Nobody had gone beyond the second-story landing, where gunsmoke—a heap of gunsmoke—still swirled from the open door of the honeymoon suite down the gaslit hall.

The asshole-puckering job of entering the smoke-filled room behind a badge as well as a drawn gun was left to the amiable Marshal White and his senior deputy, Virgil Earp. By the time they arrived, the snow white black powder smoke had thinned to where they could see all those bodies spread out bloody and dead on the pile carpet.

There were seven of them, most known at least to howdy by the town law. Old Fred White was more mystified by who might have done what, with what and, for Pete's sake, *how*!

Trigger Tanner lay sprawled by the doorway with his six-gun holstered and his face torn to shreds by a shotgun blast. It appeared the second barrel had been aimed at poor old Trigger's privates by a person or persons unknown who'd had a distinct aversion to the Texican.

All the others had been finished off with one or two shots, mostly to their chests. Turning to his deputy, White said, "See if you can find any guests who were up on this floor when all this happened, Virgil."

As Earp turned to carry out his canvass, a dishwasher from the kitchen below barged in to shout, "Chad Denton, our night bellhop, out back between the kitchen door and the stable! They got Chad, too! Dead as a turd in a milk bucket, with a big hole in his head!"

Earp said he'd go have a look-see. White shook his head and warned him, "Let's try and eat this apple a bite at a time. Dead man out back ain't as likely to leave the premises in all this confusion. Want you to tally me a list of possible witnesses that can still light out on us. Get all their names. Check names they give you against how they signed as they checked in earlier. Then ask 'em . . . Hell, Virgil, you know what to ask 'em!"

Earp allowed he did and left as White hunkered down to the grimmer task of frisking freshly shot-up bodies for personal IDs.

Thus the Great Garrick was gazing out his rear window at the confusion in the tricky light below when there came a firm knock upon his hired door.

The killer opened up with a puzzled smile to ask a tall dark lawman in rusty black what was going on.

Virgil Earp tersely replied, "I was hoping *you* might shed more light on that. I'd be Deputy Marshal Earp, and you'd be . . . ?"

"Churchward, Elmo Churchward out of Montgomery, Alabama," replied the Great Garrick in an accent he'd never heard growing up.

The less cheerful-looking Virgil Earp's tone was level but friendly as a slate walk on a cold November morn as he replied, "I was with an Illinois outfit from start to finish, but I ain't here to swap war stories. Seven men lie dead in that honeymoon suite down the hall, and I understand there's a hotel worker lying dead out back. Your turn, Mister Churchward."

The killer, faking a southern accent, smiled boyishly and asked, "Is that what I've been trying to figure out? First I heard all these gunshots—up on this floor, I think—and then another one out back. I've been trying to make out what all that shifty light and shouting out back might mean. They seem to be fussing over somebody dressed like a bellhop, stretched out in the backyard. You say you have *eight* bodies, all told, to account for?"

"That's about the size of it," the town law replied in a dismissive way to an obvious asshole who wasn't fixing to offer much help.

Hearing his name called from down the hall, the lawman who'd served with the Union Volunteers thanked the twirpy "southerner" for nothing much and headed back to the scene of the crime, as the cold-blooded criminal who'd left them such a horrible scene shut the door after him with a self-satisfied smirk.

The Great Garrick knew what the small-town lawman thought of him. He'd worked at planting the thoughts in Earp's head after hearing around town how testy the Union vet and his Scotch clan could get with Texas riders

5

inclined to brag on riding with Sibley or Hood. He'd known that acting like a simp with fetch-me-a-julep ways would inspire the total contempt of a man who'd seen the elephant in his day. That was why they called it *acting*. A man behaving *natural* wanted other men to respect him and think he was sort of smart. It took some talent to come across as a harmless dolt when you knew you were the most dangerous if not the smartest hard case for miles.

That was why the Great Garrick had styled himself after the original if not quite as great David Garrick of the English stage, who'd died sometime around the American Revolution with one and all agreed he was the greatest damned actor who'd ever trod the boards.

In his day the real Great Garrick had been famous for his quick changes as he'd played more than one part in the same play, with most of the folk out front none the wiser. They marveled at how he'd been able to get away with no more than a change of wig or, say, the robe he'd been wearing over the same shirt and vest to turn himself from Romeo for one scene into the imperious duke laying down the law about all this damned dueling near the end. They said he could fool Jews into thinking he was Shylock with little more than a fake beard and sounds that might have been muttered Hebrew. He only sounded that way when he was being Shylock. So who could be certain?

The Great Garrick's skill, as a lesser acting instructor had explained in that college class to a youth who'd been neither David Garrick nor Elmo Churchward, lay in his ability to make others think they were looking at someone else entirely by using no more than a few natural movements that took a heap of practice before a mirror and a few simple "properties," such as a bellhop's jacket of another pattern, bought in another town before coming to Tombstone, with the overall color and those shiny brass buttons, which, by gaslight, was enough to get one by as long as one *acted* the way bellhops have always acted, including the fresh mouth one *expected* from an innocent one being badgered for no sensible reason.

There'd been no call to change his dark pants and boots since he'd lit out from that honeymoon suite with all the money all those suckers had been out to win off one another. Simply replacing the jacket that no survivors could have pointed out with the *smoking* jacket he now lounged about in had been enough to change a man who'd hired a room just down the hall into a guest in a room just down the hall. Anyone could see the bellhop he'd killed in advance with a hammer blow and shoved out the rear window had been shot by the killer as he, she or it fled the premises by way of the backyard.

Since nobody else had been there, who was going to tell the law how easy it had been to lure a bellhop packing a tray into his own room, pop him with that ball-peen hammer and carry the tray on down the hall as the bellhop lay dead on the rug? The essence of the Great Garrick's skill, as he saw it, lay in rehearsal, rehearsal, rehearsal, in advance, so that when the time came to go on stage, your audience saw only what you wanted them to see, and those chumps down the hall had been so easy, for all that bullshit with Texas Rangers and prearranged signals.

Knowing before he arrived in Tombstone about those payday games on the second floor of the Cosmopolitan, the Great Garrick had plotted every bit of stage business in advance, knowing up front how his audience could be expected to respond to his every move.

Now that he'd rung down the curtain on *that* audience he had only to perform his second act for the town law to get away clean with all the money!

He knew as he sat there by the open window, tamping tobacco into a contemplative briar while staring down at the bustle below, that the Tombstone law would have possed up and set up roadblocks to prevent the escape of whomever they pictured running for it with smoking guns and gunnysacks of money.

The killer just down the hall who *had* the money, as well as other evidence, hidden above the false ceiling of that corner closet he'd had a carpenter fashion in another town for his "nearby ranchhouse," knew bulk was going to be the same pain in the ass it always was. But unlike the fleeing felon the local law imagined, the Great Garrick had plenty of time to spare.

When, not if, they got around to double-checking other guests at the Cosmopolitan, they'd find Mister Church- ward had, the first day of his stay in Tombstone, opened negotiations for the purchase of that lot on the edge of town, with a view, perhaps, to establishing a livery busi- ness out yonder, if things panned out as he hoped.

This stage business gave him plenty of time to get rid of properties he didn't want found on him as he was leav- ing or after he'd left. Small-town lawmen could be so sneaky about last-minute pat-downs of a departing sus- pect.

Allowing some time for things to cool down, the Great Garrick meant to send the money he'd made off with, in modest bundles, to a post office box he'd leased in another part of the West under another name. He meant to cut off those brass buttons and sort of lose them along Freemont Street after sunset before he ripped the livery jacket and simply left it in an alley trash can to be carted away or perhaps salvaged by some hobo. It hardly mattered, once the ruined jacket had been rendered nondescript.

With no material evidence on him or left behind, that false closet top would be nothing more than a square of hardboard left against any alley fence, and the Great Gar- rick would be free to exit stage left to no applause after discovering there were already more than enough livery operations in Tombstone for the moment.

So within days they'd have forgotten he'd ever been

by, and once again the Great Garrick would have pulled off a perfect crime.

It made him feel so smart he wanted to give himself a big wet kiss.

He knew he'd have to settle for jerking off, once he'd calmly smoked at the window a spell to show the lawmen below he was interested but not all that excited. There was no way a lone wolf plotting such perfect crimes could risk pillow talk with local gals who just might remember him.

The Great Garrick was too slick by half to leave lasting impressions as he made sure he pulled each and every job in a different jurisdiction. His simple way of leaving no witnesses to his acting ability tended to get local lawmen all hot and bothered. But as long as you never gave them the bare bones of more than one such robbery to work with, what could such a gaggle of geese do with what they had?

The Great Garrick had decided early on never, ever to pull off a job that might draw the attention of such outfits as the Pinkertons, or, God forbid, those coast-to-coast federal marshals.

So the Great Garrick had no way of knowing, as he trimmed his lamp to go to bed with his friendly hand, that this time he'd made one bodacious mistake.

For even as he pleasured himself as reward for a job well done, Marshal White was over at the nearby Western Union, getting off an all-points as regarded one of the Great Garrick's victims. His name had been Ward Redfern. He'd been wanted serious by the federal government for helping his own self to a whole lot of money entrusted to him by the Bureau of Indian Affairs, and old Fred White figured they'd want to know about all this more recent shit.

9

Chapter 2

The antique philosophers who'd observed the mills of gods and governments grind exceedingly slow and exceedingly fine had been right about the slow part. For with one dispute about jurisdicticion followed by yet another, with both wrapped up in red tape, another payday had come and gone by the time anybody asked Deputy U.S. Marshal Custis Long of the Denver District Court how he felt about events down Tombstone way.

Longarm, as he was better known by friend and foe around the Denver Federal Building or along the Owlhoot Trail, had a rep for solving posers, and it had been generally agreed there was just no sensible answer to the apparently impossible mystery of the Cosmopolitan Massacre, as it was now described in the *Tombstone Nugget*, published by Democrats; in the *Tombstone Epitaph*, published by Republicans; and in papers large and small across the land. The U.S. Marshal's Office in Tucson, the Sheriff's Department of Cochise County and even Marshal White's senior deputy were unable to buy old Fred White's picture of two or more gunslicks barging in behind a room service delivery by the late Chad Denton. For that left unexplained the finding of the bellhop's body

10

out in the backyard, minutes after the gunplay up in that honeymoon suite.

Each and every one of the rival lawmen refusing to buy Marshal White's version had his own notion as to how one busts in on an invite-only poker game to nail seven armed men before even one of them can slap leather. None of them worked any better than old Fred White's.

Longarm had read every one of the newspapers, along with government wanted flyers, plus War Department and BIA records the government had had no call to release to the fool papers. So he was as informed about the Cosmopolitan Massacre as anyone else who hadn't been there as he entered the smoke-filled inner sanctum of his superior, Marshal Billy Vail, on a cold gray morning after a prosperous but next to sleepless payday evening.

As Longarm lit a three-for-a-nickel cheroot in self-defense, the older, shorter and way fatter Billy Vail glanced up through the fumes of his own expensive but dreadful cigar to ask, "What happened to you last night? You look like you've been drug through the keyhole backwards, old son. I hope if her husband came home early you didn't have to kill him!"

Vail had never in human memory invited any of his help to sit in the horsehair-stuffed leather chair on Longarm's side of the cluttered desk. So Longarm just helped himself to a seat, shifting the cross-draw rig under his tobacco tweed coattails to ride easier on that side as he answered factually, "Business before pleasure. You don't pay me enough to endanger the husbands of white women. So I have to make up the difference over to the back room at the Black Cat whilst there's still money to be made that way."

Billy Vail sternly remarked, "Custis, you are supposed to be a peace officer, not a crooked gambler for Gawd's sake!"

11

To which Longarm calmly replied, "Don't have to crook greener hands in a friendly little game of Honest Injun poker. Only have to read faces and savvy human nature. I came out pretty good last night, and never cheated nobody. Man who can't keep a straight face with a good hand or refrain from openly weeping when he's been dealt a bad one don't deserve to leave the table with all the money he came in with."

Flicking tobacco ash on the rug, Longarm continued, "You never told old Henry out front to send me back here so you could disapprove of my payday night poker, right?"

Vail answered, "Wrong, and watch where you scatter those fucking ashes. Recalling how you and so many others seek to augment your wages with a far from friendly little game of cards, I would like to hear just how you read the demise of the late Ward Redfern down Tombstone way last month."

Longarm shrugged and flicked more ash, replying, "He was murdered and robbed by a person or persons unknown after running off from the Mescalero Agency with all those operational and allotment funds. If you don't buy my notion that tobacco ash is good for carpet mites you really ought to study on an ashtray somewhere over this way."

Vail said, "Never mind the fucking carpet mites. How do you figure an armed man who'd killed his Apache more than once wound up so dead with a Colt Lightning almost setting in his lap?"

Longarm shrugged and observed, "That Trigger Tanner guarding the one way in or out with a Schofield .45 rode with both the Texas Rangers and Hood's Brigade in his day. The professional hosting the game, the late Honest John Krebbs, rid earlier in the Mexican War, and on those occasions he encountered sore losers over many a year, since Honest John always won."

12

He treated himself to a sweeter drag on his less pungent smoke, fed the carpet mites more ash and continued, "All but one of the others at the table that evening served in the military, whether in peace or war, and must have known *something* about the guns every damned one of them had on as they lay dead on the damned rug."

Vail nodded his bullet head and said, "I read the same transcripts. Not a one of 'em got his gun out in time. According to the Cochise County coroner's findings, all seven of 'em were killed with .41-caliber slugs from the same cap-and-ball casting kit. Tanner was killed with a round of the same and finished off with modest charges of birdshot, fired point blank from close in, likely from a 16-gauge fowling piece. Take her from there, old son."

Longarm soberly replied, "Don't see where *there* might be. When I first came to work out here this crusty old fart who broke me in as a lawman told me you have to start a house of cards on a solid surface. He warned me how, once you commence to lean one card against the other in midair, they all fall down as soon as you let go."

Vail nodded approvingly and wistfully replied, "Seems like yesteryear, don't it? So what do we have that's solid and for-sure enough to commence some damned *building,* damn it?"

Longarm said, "Eight dead men. Seven in one room with .41-caliber slugs in 'em. One out back with a hole in his head that bothers me some."

Vail asked, "How come? Don't you buy Fred White's notion the killer bumped into that poor bellhop out back as he was fleeing the scene of his crime? I follow your drift about unusual head wounds. Coroner says that one old boy might have been killed with a crowbar, hammer or such because when they probed for the bullet there was no bullet to be found. But what difference does it make? Are you suggesting somebody *else* killed that bellhop out back?"

13

Longarm shrugged and said, "How do we know the killer left the hotel that evening? None of the other guests canvassed by White or his deputies could offer shit about the appearance or escape route of the one or more who busted up that poker game and lit out with all the money. We have to keep an open mind until we get some handle on which way who went with what, see?"

Vail muttered, "Me and my big mouth. Are we supposed to entertain the notion somebody *else* could have had it in for, say, a fellow employee and took advantage of the confusion to . . . what?"

Longarm warned, "You're leaning cards against cards, way in the middle of the air! When I suggest we keep an open mind I mean we have to remember we just *don't know* what happened down that way, as yet."

Glancing at the banjo clock on the oak-paneled wall, Longarm wistfully asked, "You're sending me down to find out, in Arizona Territory, with high summer coming on?"

Vail shook his head and said, "Not hardly. I figured before we had this talk that trail was cold as a banker's heart. I only wanted to hear you tell me I was right about the boys down Tombstone way missing something that may be lost forever now."

Longarm nodded and said, "What happened with nobody surviving to tell us what happened is as easy to read now as a blackboard erased by the only ones who ever read what was written on it. The killer or killers got away or made it look as if they got away before any lawman got there. I don't know how they got clear of that room with what must have added up to a carpetbag of specie and paper money. I don't know why they're using cap-and-ball ammunition on every occasion, whether that's a clue or a red herring dragged deliberate across their getaway. Is there any point to this conversation, boss? For if there ain't, it's going on quitting time, and now that I can

14

afford it there's this new gal in town who's never been out to Cherry Hill to watch the moon rise from a hired buggy and—"

"I'm sending you to Santa Fe this evening," Billy Vail cut in, adding, "Learning from past mistakes, the local and federal authorities cordoned off the scene of the crime as the gunshots were still reverberating in the wee small hours. None of the guests or hired help have been allowed to leave La Posada de San Francisco on Cathedral Place. Better yet, the sprawl butts against the Rio Santa Fe, where there ain't no bridge!"

Longarm had been to Santa Fe more than once. Noting the look in his gun-muzzle gray eyes, Billy Vail quickly added, "Well, sure a suspect all that anxious to slip away could wade the modest Rio Santa Fe at low water. But wouldn't that make him suspicious as all get-out?"

Longarm conceded, "I'd surely ask him why he was splashing about like so. What happened at La Posada de San Francisco, boss?"

Vail said, "About the same as happened down Tombstone way, only more recent. Wire came in this afternoon. Governor Wallace has asked for you in particular by name. Whilst you were playing for lower stakes at the Black Cat last night, a serious sport called Bustout Sosa, an Anglo-Mex like Pedro Maxwell—the sheep baron of Fort Sumner—hosted a serious poker game on the top floor of that sort of fancy posada along the riverside. Nobody can say exactly what happened. But along about midnight all hell busted loose up yonder and as the smoke cleared old Bustout, his doorman and half a dozen sporting gents of mixed ancestry but considerable worth lay dead on the floor with their pockets empty and their holsters still full of undischarged weaponry."

Longarm whistled and mused, "Same . . . whatever! How about hired help this time?"

Vail said, "None. This one gal working out of the can-

15

tina down below tells us she saw nothing unusual going on upstairs the last time she served coffee and tacos to old Bustout and his seven suckers."

Longarm flicked more ash and said, "Hold on—did you just say *seven*? I thought I heard you say half a dozen earlier."

Billy Vail beamed at his erstwhile student and senior deputy as he chortled, "You did, and the *escribadero* downstairs who cleared all their written invitation recalled the officious number of suckers as six. Makes you wonder, don't it?"

Longarm rose, saying, "I got a night train to catch. You say I've been given the highball from the governor's palace down yonder?"

Vail nodded and said, "From Lew Wallace in the flesh. Says he cottoned to the way you handled that bullshit down around Roswell that time. Says you showed good judgment when old rivals left over from that Lincoln County mess tried to distract you from that plain and simple stock theft along the Pecos a spell back. There's been some . . . ugly words about this latest trouble, with remarks about fucking greasers and *gringos chingados,* if you follow my drift."

Longarm sighed wearily and said, "I do. There's always talk like that where Old Mexico and New Mexico compete for fame and fortune in a land of little rain."

Vail said, "Mention was made, down Santa Fe way, of your uncanny ways with redskins, niggers and spics. How come you get along so well with redskins, niggers and spics, Custis?"

"Just a natural gift, like cinching a packsaddle on an army mule, I reckon. I found out early on it was easier when you refrained from beating a mule without a sensible reason. I got to go out front and ask Henry to type me up some travel orders."

Vail said, "No you don't," as he rummaged through

the clutter on his desk, confiding, "Had Henry whip 'em up whilst you were down the hall pulling courtroom duty this afternoon."

"That was mighty big of you, boss," Longarm dryly remarked as he accepted the sheaf of onionskin carbon copies.

Vail innocently replied, "Knew there wasn't any earlier direct connection, and what the hey, you'd have only wound up visiting a lady friend had we given you the afternoon off."

Longarm never asked whether the intent had been to preserve his health or make certain he caught that train just after sundown. He never asked if he was required to dress like an infernal sissy in a regulation suit and tie on a field mission with high summer coming in. Gents who asked when they didn't have to deserved the answers they were likely to get.

So, without asking Longarm left work early and went home to his hired digs on the unfashionable side of Cherry Creek to change into more casual riding duds and gather up his army McClellan with his saddle gun, saddlebags and possibles.

Once he had, he toted the load over to the nearby Union Station, where, seeing he had plenty of time to kill, he checked his load and ambled into the depot's fanciest dining room to treat himself to a set-down-soup-to-nuts supper.

Hence Reporter Crawford of the *Denver Post* caught Longarm in an expansive mood when he asked his permit to join him at his corner table.

The almost as tall but way beefier reporter in a too-tight checkered suit nearly blew it by asking right out whether Longarm was headed down New Mexico way to cover the Posada de San Francisco Massacre.

But Longarm really wanted to know what they had on

the wire that evening, so he calmly asked what his old newspaper pard had heard about all that.

As a waitress dressed something like a penguin with the white parts mostly apron came to take their orders, Crawford was saying, "Same as those other times in Fort Worth, Omaha, and who knows where else. The fiend seems to combine homicidal mania with the gift of invisibility! Opinion stands divided on how many times or just where he may have pulled the same nasty stunt. Dead men tell no tales, and lots of stuff goes unreported by houses of ill repute when no complaints are ever filed."

The waitress stammered, "If you gents are having *that* sort of private conversation I'd best come back later. Wave a napkin or fire a gun when you're ready to order."

Longarm soothed, "We weren't talking dirty around a lady, miss. We were talking about a homicidal maniac who murders and robs other gents, see?"

She primly replied, "Oh, in that case pray continue. I only want it known I am too proper by half to hear about anything really *wicked*!"

Chapter 3

The Colonial Spanish in their infinite wisdom never figured on such important future cities as Denver, Cheyenne and such to the north, and so they'd established their outpost of the holy faith, or Santa Fe, on a swell site at an awkward angle to the future Denver & Rio Grande Railroad.

The railroaders in their infinite wisdom had tried pretending Santa Fe wasn't there until so many potential paying passengers asked to go there that a jury-rigged rail connection was worked out. You had to transfer to the short-line Santa Fe Southern at Lamy, west of Glorieta Pass, for the last hour or so of your pilgrimage to a bodacious cluster of old churches. But you got to ride most of the way on the main line, and that took overnight and then some. So once he was aboard and they were on their way, Longarm scouted up a conductor he knew to bet him a dollar they didn't have them an empty compartment a gent riding free on a D&RGRR pass could flop in as the night wore on.

Old Gus said he'd settle for one of them fine three-for-a-nickel smokes Longarm was so generous with. Old Gus had been the conductor the night that gang of loco desperados had tried to board the train over the observation platform by way of the club car where Longarm had been washing down a Ned Buntline thriller with a needled beer. Gus allowed old Longarm had sure been more than welcome aboard *that* night.

They both knew Longarm knew his way up or down the swaying railcars, so Gus just slipped him the key to a compartment up ahead and went on about his ticket-punching once they'd parted friendly.

It was way too early for a born night owl to settle in for the night. But he lugged his heavy baggage—in a form invented by General George B. McClellan—from above his original coach car seat to lock away in the right cozy or sort of stuffy Pullman compartment at his disposal.

The load was heavy but in one handy piece, because though old George had been a failure as a field commander, he'd been one hell of a quartermaster, who, just in time for the war, designed one hell of an army saddle, based on an Austro-Hungarian cavalry saddle old George had admired and improved upon, a lot. The McClellan saddle was easier on the horse than most, if a tad less comfortable for an unskilled rider, and, best of all to the needs of the Indian Fighting Army or a lawman riding rough in the field, old George had studded his invention with brass fixtures you could lash all sorts of shit to, solid.

Hence, as Longarm stored his load on a compartment shelf, he secured his Winchester '73 saddle gun, capacious saddlebags full of shit, four empty canteens (water weighing eight pounds a gallon and pumps being handy lots of places one might light out across a desert from), with, of course, his bedroll, wrapped around a core of canned grub and lashed across the saddlebags behind the higher-than-English cantle.

This Canadian Mountie he'd worked with had opined that Yankee cavalry saddles looked sort of cowboy, in his opinion. Longarm had cheerfully agreed that was likely why so many dudes fell off while riding English flat saddles.

Though it was tempting, Longarm was too well traveled to crack open the grimy window of the stuffy compartment; he knew it was grimy because the engine up ahead burned soft coal. He also knew that the heat the compartment had soaked up earlier that day would give way to the need for those blankets by his usual bedtime. You couldn't tell with the scenery already so dark out yonder, but they were rolling a mile above sea level across the aprons of the higher Rocky Mountains to their west, and as hot as the days might get out this way, most nights were cool to downright freezing the year around.

Having secured his shit, Longarm ambled on back to the club car, paying no mind to some of the stares he attracted. You could tell recent arrivals from folk who'd been out West a spell by the way they stared at a man only dressed for the occasion aboard a train that got robbed from time to time.

Longarm wasn't gussied up fancy as some of the old boys on the covers of a Ned Buntline thriller. His telescoped black-coffee Stetson rode Cavalry slant with nothing in the way of rattlesnake hatbands or Mex fly tassels. His dark hair was perhaps a tad long by military standards but it hardly dangled down to his shoulders as if he thought he were Buffalo Bill or a poet. He made no apologies for his manly but sensible mustache.

The dark bandanna he'd replaced his shoestring tie with was knotted neat and his hickory work shirt was only two buttons open from the top under a sun-faded but clean denim bolero jacket.

If the jacket failed to hide his double-action Colt .44-40 as well as did the infernal frock coat they made him wear around the federal building, it was a factory-finished tool of his trade with no fancy silver inlays or high-toned ivory grips, and it rode in a utilitarian holster meant more for a fast draw than for show.

Many a smirk-face seemed to consider Longarm better than tall and he'd gotten mighty tired of being asked how the weather was up where he was. He would have stood taller had he favored the high heels many range riders stomped about in. But as a lawman who never knew when he might find himself fighting on foot, Longarm walked tall in the low-heeled army stovepipes he'd first stepped into, and walked a ways, as a teenaged West-by-God-Virginia boy invited to that war they were giving in his honor. Longarm could run in those stout stovepipes faster than the boy he'd been could have managed barefoot and, better yet, you didn't have to worry about busted glass or horse shit when you were wearing army boots.

Not swaggering, but unconsciously filling the aisles and doorways with his self-confident stride as he made his way back, Longarm was not aware of the way he seemed to dominate the doorway as he entered the club car of the clickety-clacking night train. The bar ran along the right side, nearer the front. You could find a seat and one of the colored boys would come to take your order for you. But Longarm paused at the bar to howdy the colored barkeep he knew and ask if they still served that fine Denver draft needled with Maryland rye.

Once he'd established they did, Longarm toted his own schooner to one of the vacant seats farther back and set it on the bitty round table bolted to the floor with such occasions in mind. There was nothing else on there as he took a seat. He had, of course, made note of what seemed to be seated next to it, but the night was young and a traveling man who started up with a pretty stranger on a train was hardly a well-traveled man.

A kindly older soldier, grateful to a kid who'd saved his ass at Shiloh, had imparted words of wisdom Longarm had been forever grateful for during that three-day leave in Nashville.

After watching a healthy teenager a long way from home acting foolish as hell around women who kept laughing at him, the older and way wiser pal had sat young Private Long down for some fatherly advice on the art of getting laid.

As that old-timer had intoned and as Longarm had found to be the case ever since, it was simply not true that men chased after women. Not men who wound up in bed with them, leastways.

His mentor, now long-dead—they'd blow his head off at Lookout Mountain—had confided, "A natural woman has made up her mind by the time she's had her eye on you five minutes whether she'd like you to fuck her or not. But that don't mean she's *certain*. All sorts of wrong moves can change her mind before you've come up with flowers, books or candy. A heap of men blow their chances on an easy lay by spooking the object of their desire. So the first move you want to learn is letting *her* make the first damn move. If she don't fancy you, nothing you can do or say is going to get you some action and you're just wasting your pocket jingle and youth on a lost cause."

The older man, who did seem to have a way with the ladies, had added in a confidential tone, "On the other hand, if she *does* fancy you, there ain't a thing you have to do but take your beating like a man, *as long as you don't blow it* with any move that wrinkles her pretty little nose!"

The peaches and cream blonde seated next to him had a pretty little nose indeed, peeking out through a lace veil of the perky summer straw perched atop her upswept goldy locks. He couldn't make out her eyes, as they seemed to be avoiding his. She had a tan poplin travel duster on over whatever else she might be wearing, no doubt for the same reasons she had half her face covered by that veil: A soft coal cinder in the eye could be a big bother, bigger even than a smudge on a new summer frock.

She sat with her legs crossed, and he couldn't say whether her nicely turned high-buttoned tootsie was moving that way because she was nervous or just bouncing in time with the clickety-clacks you could feel with your whole spine if you thought about 'em.

A million years went by as Longarm took a sip and put the schooner back on the table betwixt them. Then he saw one of the colored boys coming with one of those newfangled cocktail drinks on a serving tray and craw-fished his bigger container off the table, murmuring, "Sorry, ma'am. I fear I owe you an apology for not having better sense!"

She turned to favor him with big, warm chocolate eyes and a dimpled smile, as if noticing him there for the first time, and warmly replied, "Don't you imagine these immovable tables are meant to be shared, kind sir?"

To which he felt safe to reply, "Aw, I ain't no *sir,* ma'am. I'd be Custis Long. Riding for the Denver District Court and on my way to Santa Fe on government beeswax."

As the attendant put her drink down, she tipped him extra, then turned to the lawman to confide, "I thought I recognized you. Everybody calls you Longarm, right?"

He modestly replied, "Not everybody. Some Mexicans insist on describing me as *El Brazo Largo* whilst Mister Lo, the Poor Indian, has been known to call me *Ees ta haska.*"

She didn't follow his drift, meaning she savvied neither Spanish nor Lakota. He didn't offer to translate. Nobody liked a smart-ass, and he'd already been tempted to sort of show off.

Hoping he hadn't put his foot in it, Longarm cuddled

24

his drink up to hers on the one bitty table. The cocktail she'd ordered looked a lot like cranberry juice and smelled a lot like gin. He'd heard how women traveling where the water was uncertain swilled cranberry juice to preserve their bladders. He warned himself not to dwell on the possible bladder problems of anybody that pretty.

As if she'd read his mind, the peaches and cream vision heaved a sigh and said, "I was sort of hoping you'd be going all the way with me—to El Paso, I mean. My given name is Modesty Bevers, but my friends call me Mod. I see you don't remember me, but we were introduced at the Harvest Ball last autumn. I was appearing at the Apollo Hall in *The Flower Girls of Paris* that season."

"I figured you had to be an actress, Miss Mod," Longarm truthfully replied, knowing he'd never been introduced to any face so impossible to forget.

Mod sipped her up-to-date drink in a sissy wine goblet as Longarm went on to ask what play she might be appearing in down El Paso way.

She replied, "I'm not. I'm bound for an engagement at the Birdcage Theatre in Tombstone, if I ever get there. The train connections read awfully complicated."

He said, "You can't get there from here, or anywheres by train, Miss Mod; knowing that makes it less confusing. You only have one transfer to make, the same as me. You board the westbound Southern Pacific at El Paso and just get off at Tucson, Arizona Territory."

"Is that close to Tombstone?" she asked, hopefully.

He said, "Close as you can get by rail. You board the Tucson Bisbee stage at Tucson and get off at Tombstone eight or ten hours later, Lord willing and the creeks don't rise."

She looked as if she might be fixing to cry. So he patted her wrist and quickly added, "Flash floods are rare down yonder this time of the year, and nobody ever robs them stages outward-bound from Tucson. The few holdups they've had involved bullion rolling west to Tucson from the mines around Tombstone or Bisbee. See?"

She finished her smaller but more potent drink and raised a gloved hand to signal the barkeep as she decided, "I might just stay aboard all the way to California. I just read about a mass murder right in the middle of Tombstone. I had no idea the place was so difficult to *get* to! What's Santa Fe like, Custis?"

It was mighty tempting, but he sort of like the flighty little thing and so he said, "Much the same, complete with a more recent mass murder. They figure it was the same cold-blooded cuss. After that Santa Fe is way older and more spread out than Tombstone, but not much bigger and offering less in the way of opportunities. The few rich folk there made their money grazing stock, or since it's the capital of the territory, fleecing the sort of sheep you get to vote for you. I have to get off a shorter ways out of Santa Fe for the same reason you have to get to Tombstone by getting off at Tucson. Maybe someday, Miss Mod, but as of now there's heaps of places out this way you just can't get to the easy way."

That same colored boy brought her another whatever without having to be told what she was drinking. Longarm wasn't sure he wanted to know. He was less than halfway down his beer schooner but he ordered another to save the boy needless trouble as the steel wheels under them screeched like owls and he had to grab on to Mod lest she slide off her seat.

With a startled look in her big brown eyes, she gasped, "Good heavens, what was that all about?" once the night train began to roll on more sedately.

Longarm explained, "I 'spect we just hit a stretch of overdue repair work, Miss Mod. Tracks run south on ballast rock dumped on top of former prairie. Betwixt rotting-out grass roots and prairie dogs, the roadbed is inclined to settle uneven. So from time to time track crews come along to shift and resettle things more level."

He sipped some suds and added, "Sometimes they don't have the time for all the repairs that need tending. Most times they do. So don't let it get you flusterpated."

She said, "I fear it already has. I'm not sure whether it's all this clickety-clacking or the grenadine in these Colorado Sunsets, but I sure wish there was somewhere I could lie down aboard this noisy night train!"

Longarm cautiously asked, "Didn't you book yourself a compartment, or at least a Pullman berth, seeing you were fixing to be aboard all night and then some, Miss Mod?"

She sighed and confessed, "I wouldn't be Tombstone-bound if I still had work back there in Denver. Our tour manager skipped out and stranded us a good two weeks ago, and Denver is such an expensive town. . . ."

Longarm said he understood. He did. The question before the house was whether she'd known all along about that compartment up ahead or whether by any chance she really liked him.

Chapter 4

Like many a man before him, Longarm often found it tougher to get a gal to join him in a private place than it was to get her out of her duds once he got her there. It was the starry-eyed ones who went willingly that you had to watch out for. They were the ones most given to hurt looks and wild accusations as soon as they found themselves swapping spit in the dark with a natural man. Gals who expected a natural man to act natural were naturally more inclined to shilly-shally along the way.

Another stretch of rough roadbed helped, more ways than one. It made Mod more anxious to recline, and Longarm suspected, from the way the train slowed down, that they had more time to work with before he had to get off, win, lose or draw.

Advising her he had the makings of many a cocktail in his saddlebags up ahead, Longarm left the club car with her and a pitcher of ice. Mister George Pullman supplied running water in his private compartments, Lord love him. Unlike the less fortunate who bedded down in curtained Pullman berths, you didn't need to go out in the corridor to shit when you booked a private compartment.

He felt no call to mention this to Mod before she asked.

So she asked twenty minutes after they were alone up yonder behind a sliding door with a barrel bolt and the moonlit scenery whipping by romantically outside the clean-enough window glass.

When she shyly confessed the highball he'd fixed her made her have to heed the call of nature and added she'd heard how up-to-date these newer compartments were, Longarm gallantly raised the green plush seat pads of what looked like a built-in easy chair to expose the copper-bowled commode.

He made delicate reference to the chain hung discreetly in the angle formed by the set-down shitter and an upright wardrobe before he stepped out into the corridor to afford her some . . . delicacy.

Knowing how time dragged when you weren't having fun, he checked his pocket watch right off and resolved to afford her a quarter hour before he knocked discreetly on the sliding door.

A quarter hour didn't sound that long, but more than one fellow passenger had to work past him awkwardly, as so much of him seemed to occupy the space left for lesser beings by old George Pullman in designing his fool cars for maximum lie-down space.

When Gus the conductor caught up with him in the dimly lit corridor, he was too polite to ask what in thunder Longarm was up to. He'd seen Mod talking to Longarm earlier, back in the club car.

So Longarm stopped him with the offer of another cheroot and said, "I know I'm pushing my luck. So if this ought to cost me any money don't hesitate to say so, Gus."

Gus let Longarm light the smoke for him before he quietly replied, "I admire your taste. If we're talking about my listing that compartment as empty all the way to El Paso, it's my understanding it is, and that is how I've got things down on paper."

Longarm said, "That's mighty Christian of you, Gus. Win, lose or draw, the lady is down on her luck and—"

"I don't know what you're talking about," Gus cut in, severely adding with a poker face, "If I knew for certain the Denver & Rio Grande had an empty compartment full of ladies, I'd have to *do* something about it. Since as far as I know nobody but me has a key to that sliding door behind you, I don't have to do shit, if you follow my drift."

Longarm allowed he did and added, "I got a running bar tab at that fancy Parthenon Saloon up Denver way, next time you're up that way with a guest of your own choosing."

He pressed more smokes on the nice old cuss and added, "They got private side rooms at the Parthenon, and the cold cuts they serve with at least two beers rivals the grub in many a chili parlor."

Gus allowed he might take Longarm up on that and they parted friendly with five minutes to go, according to the lawman's infernally slow watch.

Then the sliding door behind him opened a crack and Mod's lost-little-gal voice inquired, "Do you mean to mope out there all night, Custis?"

As he rejoined her in the dimmer light from the westward-facing grimy glass, he saw she'd shucked that travel duster and then some. Shyly pointing to the neatly hung print summer frock she'd removed along with the duster, Mod confided, "I fear I've been . . . glowing inside all that calico and poplin with the air so stuffy tonight!"

He said, "It's early yet. Before midnight you'll have goose bumps if you don't watch out."

Sitting on the cot along the windows, Mod went on as if she hadn't heard him. "I hope I haven't shocked you, lounging about like this in just my chemise and stockings. Sometimes we troupers who tread the boards are inclined

30

to be more . . . practical in private than Queen Victoria approves of.

Feeling sort of overdressed, Longarm commenced to hang up his hat, his six-gun and his jacket as he replied, "I toured aboard a train with the one and original Miss Sarah Bernhardt and her French Variety Company a spell back, Miss Mod. So I know what you mean about the more casual attire worn backstage. Queen Victoria doesn't have to change from one costume to another more than once an hour."

Mod threw her blond head back to laugh and declared, "Her Majesty just doesn't know what she's missing. I read in this fashion magazine how, someday, respectable ladies would be allowed to show more leg than this, out in public. Do you think we'll ever see the day, Custis?"

He chuckled and said, "I doubt it. But one can always hope. Statues are already allowed to get by in public with no more than a fig leaf."

He sat down beside her to explain his conversation with old Gus, adding, "Long as you don't go out and leave the door unlocked, you'll be free to lounge in a state of dishabille in private all the way to El Paso. When you're ready to leave, don't pester Gus; he don't want to hear. Leave the key on this bunk as you go. Leave the door slid open an inch or so and just get off. Where did you leave your baggage in your coach car? I'll fetch it for you."

She hesitated, then said, "I boarded without any baggage, Custis. I fear my poor old steamer trunk will never escape from my hotel alive: I went out to shop for magazines owing more than three weeks' rent."

Longarm smiled thinly and decided, "Well, that's doubtless why they want you to pay up front when you check in without baggage."

She didn't answer. He chose his words thoughtfully before he told her, "I had a run of luck payday night, and

I'd likely spend most of my easy money foolish, Miss Mod. So I'd be honored if you'd let me grubstake you with a share of my winnings."

She didn't answer for a long time. When she did she asked in a colder tone if he was trying to buy her favors.

He shook his head to reply, "Perish the thought. I'm too romantical to pay for such services, no offense."

She got to her feet, murmuring, "I think I'd like to put my clothes on and go back to my coach car now. I'm sorry if my backstage ways gave you the wrong impression of a legitimate actress, good sir!"

Longarm got to his own feet to set her firmly down as he intoned in a voice of command, "Don't tell everybody how dumb you are, Miss Mod—give us a chance to guess. You are in a worse fix than I've been in for some time. But I've been there and I know the feeling. So here's what we are fixing to do. . . ."

She sobbed, "I'm not that kind of girl! I'm not! I'm not!"

He said, "We've established that. I got to leave you the key but I'll want my saddle and possibles when I get off at Lamy in the morning. So do I knock like so, I'll be obliged if you let me back in to gather up my own baggage. Do we have a deal?"

She stammered, "I guess so. I don't understand. Where will you be all that time . . . Custis?"

He got out his wallet as he replied, "Back where you found me. Put this money away and don't open up to anybody who doesn't knock like so."

As he tapped out a shave-and-a-haircut on the hardwood bulkhead, Mod got back to her feet to demand, "Are you sure? This isn't some kind of a joke? It hardly seems fair!"

To which he could only reply as he regathered his hat, jacket and six-gun, "Whoever told you things had to be fair?"

Then, as long as she was standing there, he kissed her, brotherly, and headed back to the club car whilst he still had the force of will. He'd meant what he said about not paying for it. But there'd been times he'd been tempted, and this had been one of them.

He was cussing himself considerable by the time he made it back to the club car. Missing out on a nice piece of tail wasn't going to injure his health all that much. Showing up in Santa Fe after a night sitting up with nobody to pass the time with but other sleepless gum-eyes wasn't likely to add luster to his reputation along the Owlhoot Trail, even if he went easy on the beer and pretzels. So he helped himself to a deck chair seat on the observation platform to nurse his tobacco by moonlight as the smoke-scented air currents tried to whip his hat off.

It couldn't, because he didn't want it to and knew how to wear a Stetson Cavalry style. The moon was high and he could see back up the tracks about as far as where the tracks merged to a point on the northern skyline. He was glad it wasn't raining. But that was about all he could say for the dumb way his night was turning out. It was barely ten-thirty and he was already bored stiff.

The platform door slid open behind him. Longarm wished it hadn't. He would have stayed inside at the bar if he'd wanted to engage in the sort of conversations one had with strangers on a train. But there was more than one deck chair on the platform, and he didn't own it. So he neither turned nor made any comment as somebody sat down next to him. Then a familiar voice remarked in a familiar way, "I must be a better actress than I thought. I only wanted to establish I wasn't a whore. I never expected to be taken for a *nun*!"

Longarm had to laugh before he said, "*Schoolgirl* is the word you were groping for, Miss Mod. Nobody could ever take you for a celibate nun in your shimmy shirt and silk stockings."

She sighed and said, "Stage business. Meant to imply you were in the company of a woman of the world with a backstage approach to life and . . . Didn't you say you'd spent some time backstage, with other actresses?"

He smiled fondly and answered, "French actresses. Sometimes you'd meet up with one wearing nothing at all betwixt costume changes and they'd never bat an eye as they scampered by. But after you got used to backstage life you found it wasn't all that different from life in general."

He took a last drag on his smoked-down cheroot and snuffed it out on his heel as he continued. "In my line of work you deal with acting on and off the stage. A French gal running past buck naked ain't half as shocking as a dignified church elder and bank president planning an inside job, and, at the moment, they have me on the trail of somebody so good at playacting, that he seems to be invisible."

She suggested, "Why don't you tell me all about it up in that compartment. I didn't put anything on under this duster, and it's getting chilly out here."

He stayed put as he pointed out in a more grown-up tone, "Miss Mod, you know as well as I do how much *talking* we're likely to engage in if the two of us wind up back in that compartment."

She coyly suggested they find out. So he got up and walked her back most the length of the night train, attracting no little attention from old Gus and several passengers, because Mod had left her veiled summer straw up ahead and had let her long goldy locks down for the night.

One they were back in the darker compartment, Longarm kissed her in a far less brotherly fashion than he had earlier as he helped her out of her poplin duster. That was when he realized she wasn't wearing anything but her silk stockings and high-buttons under it. So they tore off the first one atop the bedding with his shirt open, his jeans down around his boots and his six-gun grips digging into her rump; she complained, until she unbuckled the rig and let the fool .44-40 look for its own gal, anywhere it pleased.

She removed his knotted bandanna as they came up for air and suggested he take off the rest himself before they went at it some more.

He did and they did, with Mod winding up on top and marveling, "Oh my Lord! If I just hold you tight inside me like this and don't move, those clickety-clacking wheels under us make you sort of clickety-clack all over!"

He managed not to remark that he'd noticed this phenomenon on earlier occasions aboard night trains. He didn't want to hear how she'd learned to fuck so fine, and one of the dumb moves his old army mentor had warned him about was the tendency to brag about earlier conquests.

So he never did, and, wonder of wonders, after that awkward start, Mod turned out to be one of those rare women who just fucked like you'd asked her to dance, with no mention of other dance partners, dancing her good or bad around the same ballroom. Nor did she mention the money again, so they both knew she had it in some safe place.

It took only a spell of immobile clickety-clack with her clit pressed against his pubic bone to further propel her ride to the hounds, and when she missed a jump and fell off the saddle horn he rolled her onto her naked back to finish right lest she snap his poor old organ grinder like a twig.

As he pounded her to glory she stared out the grimy glass beside her pretty face to marvel, "Oh! That's the third shooting star I've seen in this position, and I'm running low on wishes!"

Longarm was too busy to answer. But after he'd come

all the way down to his curled-under toes he felt obliged
to remark, as he let it soak in her, "Them's the Perseid
meteors, Miss Mod. Get 'em every year in the dog days
of August. Mostly like tonight, a dozen or more an hour.
But now and again shooting stars come in swarms like
bees. I wasn't there, but they say back in '33 they had a
meteor shower that had folk coast to coast down on their
knees praying for deliverance whilst Mister Lo, the Poor
Indian, still says that was what wiped the Mandan Nation
out."

She thrust her naked hips out teasingly to murmur,
"Did you bring me back here to fuck me or to offer me
an astronomy lesson, you brute?"

So he laughed and got to moving in and out some more
and in no time at all he felt up to the occasion again.
When Mod asked him to tell her what was so funny, he
soothed, "Wasn't laughing at you. Something this older
gent I served in the war with just came back to me."

She wrapped her silk-sheathed legs around his bare
waist as she asked to be let in on the joke, adding in a
throaty growl that she felt sure it had to be a dirty one.

As he moved in time with the clickety-clacking steel
wheels below them, Longarm explained, "Wasn't a joke.
More like a long conversation about . . . times like these.
His name was Randall. Abe Randall. Ain't thought of Abe
for years. The last I saw of Abe, on the torn-up slopes of
Lookout Mountain, didn't leave me a memory I like to
dwell on."

"I remind you of a battlefield casualty, in this position?" she gasped.

He merely started moving in her faster; life was too
short to try talking sense with a woman. So a grand time
was had by all, and after they'd come again Mod marveled, "Oh, goody, I just saw another shooting star, and
this time I wished you'd do it to me one more time!"

He started to protest that he needed at least a couple of drags on a smoke to get his wind back. But she was still hot and he was still hard, so Private Long soldiered on, murmuring, "This one's for you, Abe!"

Chapter 5

Mod wanted to get off with Longarm at Lamy and follow him to the ends of the earth, or at least until her next period. But he pointed out that other lawmen, newspaper reporters and such would be waiting at the Santa Fe Southern station with heaps of curious townees, if not a brass band, and preserving her reputation won out over the way he made her see shooting stars. So he left her in the compartment, staring goggle-eyed at the drawn-down curtains, and got off with his duds on and the McClellan braced opposite his six-gun on his right hip to cross the platform, walking funny, and board the northbound short-line.

The eighteen- or nineteen-mile run across marginal range and stretches of pure desert took less than a full hour and, sure enough, quite a delegation was waiting for him at the station. Billy Vail's opposite number down that way, Marshal Ignacio Harris of the Santa Fe District Court, had arrived in a surrey driven by a pure Mex deputy, and this was just as well, because the smoky railroad yards sprawled a long rifle shot south of the east-to-west Santa Fe River and as far again from the central plaza where most everything important in the territorial capital could be found.

Marshal Harris, as his first name hinted, was only a tad older than Longarm, and of a type more typical to New Mexico than, say, Texas. Older Spanish land-grant families had just laughed when poor whites moving in on them after the Mexican War tried to dismiss *them* as greasers. More than one *Nuevo Mejico* grandee had owned and still owned enough land, fee simple, to fill one of the more modest Eastern states.

So on the principle that when you couldn't whip 'em it was best to join 'em, heaps of gringos, Irish Papists in particular, had married up with highborn New Mexican señoritas to produce rich politicos or rancheros with such confusing names as Pete or Pedro Maxwell, Ignacio Harris and such. Longarm knew an ambitious former buffalo hunter called Pat Garret, out of Alabama, who'd married one of the Gutierrez sisters after the other. When his first wife, Juanita, up and died on him, old Pat soldiered on with her sister, Apolinaria, and he figured on the Mex as well as the Irish vote when he ran for sheriff of Lincoln County.

Marshal Harris didn't look all that Mex. Most of the land-grant clans had started out *sangreazulo,* or blue-blooded, and married betwixt themselves. It was no longer fashionable to say so in New Mexico, but some who'd been there said no paid-up member of the KKK could hold a candle to a pure Spanish New Mexican when it came to looking down his nose at poor folk of the Hispanic persuasion and mestizo ancestry.

Their driver, alone in the seat ahead, looked more like you expected a Mex to look, although the Marshal ordered him about respectfully. Others who tagged after, once they'd shaken hands back at the railroad terminal, had been introduced as territorial and county law, with a dusting of newspapermen and pissed-off pals of the half dozen locals murdered at La Posada de San Francisco a couple of nights back.

The distance they had to cover was too far to walk in high summer but a mighty short buggy ride. So all Longarm got out of Harris along the way sounded much as Billy Vail had described the situation, and the situation was a bait can of really slimy night crawlers, which was why none of the local lawmen had raised one eyebrow over a lawman from another jurisdiction horning in.

Longarm knew from sad experience how anxious local lawmen were to use easy arrests to look good. He knew they knew they didn't look so good when they seemed to be chasing their own tails whilst the public clamored for justice. After Harris told Longarm they still had all possible suspects under house arrest at the comfortable but confined posada off to the east, he said he and the boys were open to suggestions.

By this time they'd reined in out front of the governor's palace on the main plaza, and bigger shots were expecting him inside. So as he got out with his baggage, Longarm suggested, "It's your call, Marshal. But if you were to give everyone a tad more rope, one or more of them might hang themselves. This is the first time that the same killer's pulled such a stunt up a blind alley, no offense."

Marshal Harris allowed he didn't follow Longarm's drift. The junior lawman explained, "You gents who spend a lot of time here in Santa Fe may have lost track of how tough it is to get in or out of this neck of the woods. I just got off the only rail connection with the outside world, and a stranger in these parts might be sore put to get out any other way. He'd have to hire a livery mount. After that he'd likely want to hire a guide to show him the way through the ferocious mountains surrounding all your dry range, where a strange rider stands out like a fly in one's soup."

40

Harris said he followed Longarm's drift, as he got out too. Longarm didn't ask why; it stood to reason the local federal marshal would get to 'tend most powwows in the governor's palace. Harris told his deputy driver to wait, and as they entered he called another Mex over to take charge of Longarm's awkward baggage so's the two of them could stride on to the meeting called by Governor Wallace.

The appointed American governor's palace had been built for the Spanish governors earlier, out of unmilled timber and mud, as adobe bricks were originally fashioned from. But after the old-time Spanish or the Indians they'd been bossing around had managed a right serviceable lay-out, the Americanos had taken over with pleasure. The mixture of chopped straw and clay soil *they* called adobe, from a Hispano-Moorish handle for mud bricks, dried to a warm buckskin color, and the thick walls kept the inside rooms from getting too cold in winter or too hot in summer. Mud and unmilled timber being free for the gathering amongst the headwaters of the Rio Grande, the original builders hadn't stinted on the sizes of said rooms, and the one the governor was now holding the meeting in around an acre or so of cordovan-stained oak tabletop was as big as some courtrooms Longarm had visited. Since he'd been expected, a massive armchair of Spanish design had been provided for him, with an empty glass handy at his place at the table. As he sat down, a young barefoot gal who might have been Apache filled the glass from her pitcher of sangria.

Governor Wallace, seated at the center across the long table, waited till she finished before he called the meeting to order and introduced himself to Longarm.

Longarm was too polite to mention they'd met before. Men as famous as the one and original Lew Wallace met way more folk than they could ever be expected to remember.

41

Now a quietly competent-looking man in his bearded fifties, Lew Wallace deserved to be famous. After serving with distinction in the Union Army through most of the war, he'd spent enough time in the Diplomatic Service to write a heap of his famous novel, *Ben Hur,* from personal memories of Rome and the Holy Land.

Then, about the time his swamping two-volume saga was going to press, his wartime pal, President Hayes, had called him back to federal service and appointed him governor of New Mexico Territory to replace that half-ass or crooked Governor Axtell and for Gawd's sake *do* something about the corrupt Santa Fe Ring and that mad-dog Lincoln County War.

Old Lew Wallace had gotten more famous doing both—or at least the papers said he had. Longarm could hardly have been the only one there who knew that Wallace had arrived in New Mexico months after the Lincoln County War had been won, and hence ended, by the Murphy-Dolan faction, with a few surviving Tunstall-McSween gun waddies such as Billy the Kid and the more dangerous Charlie Bowdre reduced to stealing stock for a living.

But after graciously offering an amnesty to any fighting men who'd care to stop fighting, with their war over, the new broom had swept some of the shadowy Santa Fe Ring out of the cobwebby corners of local trade and politics. Old Lew had New Mexico running about right, save for the natural if sort of high crime rate west of, say, longitude 100°, and this bullshit at La Posada de San Francisco had him off his feed and feeling futile.

Smiling wearily across the table at their outside expert, the governor asked if Longarm ever felt like poor old Sisyphus. Then he sighed and said, "I'm sorry, Deputy Long. I fear I've become one of those bookworms who forget themselves."

Longarm easily replied, "I know who Sissy Puss was,

Governor. He was that antique Greek who got in trouble with them Greek gods. So they set him to work rolling this swamping rock up a steep hill, and it took him all day to do so."

"What happened then?" asked another lawman, sporting a Mex sombrero.

Longarm said, "Every night the rock rolled all the way back down and old Sissy Puss got to start all over in the morning, rolling that pain-in-the-neck rock back up again, and so it went, forever and ever, or as long as them Greek gods were running things, leastways."

Governor Wallace smiled thinly and said, "I couldn't have put it more clearly. This so-called San Francisco Massacre is going to draw the same sort of headlines that shoot-out in Lincoln Plaza in the summer of '78 did, and just standing there with his jaw hanging open cost the man I replaced this job!"

Marshal Harris cut in with, "Me and Longarm were just now planning a move that might be worth a try. We decided that since nobody we've got pinned down near the scene of the crime seems fixing to crack, we might just turn 'em all loose, with a warning to stay in town until we tell 'em they can leave, and then see who tries to leave."

Another lawman protested, "Jesus H. Christ, Iggy, how long would *you* stick around with nobody riding herd on you if you'd just shot eight men in cold blood?"

Harris looked at Longarm. Longarm said, "Depends on how smart a killer I was. I don't think we're up against a blue streaker who runs for the woodwork like a cockroach. He's taken about the same brutal but simple approach at least a dozen times, far and wide over a period of eighteen months. I was going over the transcripts as I rode up from Lamy earlier. Until he did away with that federal want in Tombstone and helped himself to government funds, he's left a fuzzy trail indeed, with lawmen in many a jurisdiction never comparing notes."

The lawman in the big hat nodded it, an awesome sight, and said, "That's my point, Denver Boy. Since nobody knows who he might be or what he might look like, he could be any one of the guests and hired help we've got to work with over to the posada, and I tally close to thirty suspects in all!"

Longarm said, "If it was the work of the same killer, we're not dealing with anything like thirty suspects. Unless folk known to reside in or about Santa Fe can be shown to have been out of town during any of those *other* messy robberies . . ."

Marshal Harris said, "Hot damn! That's what I meant! If the murderous two-face shot up that other poker game in Tombstone last month, he has to be a new arrival, meaning a *total stranger* up our way! We can 'liminate all the hired help at the posada as well as anybody ever registered there in the past, or able to explain what he, she or it was doing there the other night!"

Another local lawman, who looked more Mex, said, "I can tell you without having to ask any of 'em. Folk with kith and kin nearby don't check into transient lodgings. I've talked to every blamed one of them posada guests. One of 'em has to be lying like a rug, of course. But how do you tell your average mad-dog killer from a whiskey drummer, a bobwire salesman or a lunger whose doctor advised the air out our way, if the only one lying is a really good liar?"

Harris said, "The more reson to give them all some rope. Honest folk with honest business in these parts are going to just go on about their honest business. Meanwhile we stake out the one railroad terminal and all the livery stables in town."

The Mexican hat nodded thoughtfully and said, "We ask all the barkeeps and barbers to keep us informed of strangers in town who might ask about a saddle mount or

44

buggy for hire, say for a day trip to admire those pueblos up Taos way?"

Governor Wallace said, "I don't know. At the risk of sounding erudite, you know what they say about a bird in the hand, and no offense, but none of you seem to be able to locate stock thieves we know by name as they scamper through the chaparral all around!"

And so the meeting went, as such meetings often did, with nothing decided one way or the other as siesta time approached.

So in the end it was agreed they just leave things as they were for now, and as they broke up for La Siesta, Marshal Harris invited Longarm to come stay with him and his *mujer* not far away.

Longarm said, "I thank you for the neighborly invite, Marshal. But I figured, long as I'm here and the scene of the crime I'm here on seems to be a popular posada, I might as well check in *there* for now."

Harris started to argue. But he'd heard that Longarm was a sneaky devil who played with his cards close to his vest. So when they got outside Harris told his driver to scout up Longarm's baggage and drive him over by the river to La Posada de San Francisco, adding he meant to leg the shorter distance to his own place and let his driver drive his ownself home for La Siesta.

So the mestizo, Bob for Roberto, was in a good mood as they drove east to the big 'dobe cathedral of the Santa Fe de San Francisco, or Holy Faith of Saint Francis.

As they swung south, Bob crossed himself and confided a secret known mostly only to the older and poorer population thereabouts. The imposing Saint Francis Cathedral on all those postcards was nigh brand-new, built by the recent Archbishop Lamy they'd named that railroad stop for, albeit they had the oldest statue of the Virgin Mary in North America in one of their chapels inside.

Bob held, and Longarm had no call to argue, that the

oldest church of all in Santa Fe was San Miguel's, built five years after those pilgrims landed on Plymouth Rock by Tlaxcalan masons brought north from Old Mexico. Bob bragged some of his Tanoan *mamacita*'s kin to the north lived in the oldest city in the present United States. Longarm didn't doubt him. He'd heard Taos was pretty old.

He was too polite to suggest it was about time they paved at least the main streets in those parts.

Cathedral Road hadn't been. But they only raised a little dust driving along it to the sprawling 'dobe complex along the Santa Fe River, a most often shallow tributary of the Upper Rio Grande to the west.

Posada was usually translated as "inn" in English. The term was used more loosely by Mexicans for anything from a room-for-let over a cantina to a sort of half-ass summer resort such as La Posada de San Francisco. It was roomy and well appointed by hotel standards, albeit, like the rest of Santa Fe, mostly, if solidly, constructed of sun-baked mud.

A darker, barefoot Mex dashed out to take Longarm's McClellan away from Bob whilst another took charge of Longarm to lead him into the cool and spacious lobby. As he signed in at the desk, with an older *posadero* in a suit and tie beaming at him, Longarm couldn't help noticing another Anglo staring at him from a nearby archway. Men who stared that way at a grown man wearing a .44-40 were either spoiling for a fight or too stupid to be let out of the house without a leash.

Speaking Spanish as best he knew how, Longarm explained to the older and dignified-looking *posadero* who he was and what he was doing on the premises. The innkeeper agreed it made sense for a lawman with neither kith nor kin in these parts to check into the best posada in town, even if it *was* the scene of a crime.

Longarm allowed that since it was going on siesta time

he'd just grab a bite in their *comedor*. The older man directed him through the archway that other cuss was standing in. As he brushed past Longarm nodded and murmured, " 'Scuse me, pard."

As he went on in to find others lounging around a more informal dining area than he'd expected, serving themselves from a steam table buffet, the hard-eyed stranger in the archway followed. Seeing he seemed the object of collective interest, Longarm ticked his hat brim to the ladies and gents staring up at him to say, "Howdy, folks. I'd be Deputy U.S. Marshal Custis Long, and I'll be staying here too a spell."

The hard case just to his rear declared in a more certain tone, "He's likely another government Jew boy working for Lew the Jew Wallace!"

Chapter 6

"I was wondering if you spoke Spanish," said Longarm in that language as he turned to face the rude cuss. He'd replied to the insulting remarks in Spanish because the four she-male guests in sight seemed Anglo. The man who'd called him a Jew boy was tall, lean and mean-looking, in a black suit, maroon brocade vest and pearl gray Spanish hat. He looked to be about forty, which was long in the tooth for such a reckless mouth.

When he looked surprised but didn't answer, Longarm continued in such border Spanish as he could muster, "I cannot speak for the faith of Governor Wallace. I was sprinkled Christian, grew up with an open mind and if it might help you make up *your* mind, *Hare Krishna,* you son of a one-legged whore and dog of uncertain pedigree!"

One of the older and more proper-looking Anglo ladies seated at one table with a younger one piped up, "If you please, young sir, there are ladies present!"

Longarm asked for her pardon in Spanish without taking his eyes from the cuss in the Spanish hat, or the Colt Navy conversion with staghorn grips peeking out from under his black coattails. Then Longarm switched back to

English to softly suggest, "It's your call, pilgrim!"

The older armed man blustered, "You know very well I dasn't throw down on a self-declared federal deputy!"

Longarm nodded and replied, "Just as you knew I'd never draw first when you shot off your fat mouth. If you ain't up to my invite to draw first, I sure would like to help myself to some of them tamales and tostados I'm smelling, for I somehow missed my breakfast this morning."

Nobody trying to stop him, Longarm strode on to the steam table and found a platter with some tableware at one end. Any hired help on the far side had already lit out for La Siesta. Longarm knew that was why they were serving buffet style at the usual Anglo dinnertime. The two ways of life met each other halfway in New Mexico Territory.

There were worse ways to run things.

Piling his platter with limp moist tamales, crunchy tostados and three tortillas to sop up the sauce, Longarm carried his main entree to one of the empty tables, set it there with his doffed Stetson and tableware and went back to pour himself a big clay mug of coffee. Trying to tote all he wanted in one trip could have resulted in a spill. That was why they called such half-ass attempts a *lazy fool's load.*

As he swung around to set with his back to the 'dobe wall, that galoot in the black suit was standing there, looking awkward and tongue-tied.

Longarm quietly informed him in Spanish that his apology was accepted.

The loudmouth attempted a hearty smile, not a pretty sight, and told Longarm in a false-friendly voice, "If I was wrong about you being a Jew, I'm sorry. I had no right to take it out on you even if you were a Jew. All of us here are sore vexed with Lew the Jew Wallace for holding us here on false charges, see?"

Longarm hadn't hoped to interview any witnesses before La Siesta was over. He nodded and pointed at the empty seat across the bare blue table with a forkful of tamale as he replied, "It's my understanding nobody here has been charged with anything. All you guests as well as the staff on duty the night before last are being held as material witnesses or as folk who might light out before they give evidence."

As the other man sat down, Longarm added, "I suspect Governor Wallace may be a Scotch Presbyterian."

The material witness who thought otherwise protested, "Every blamed one of us has submitted depositions in triplicate about the little any of us know about that late night gunplay upstairs, and if Lew the Jew ain't a Jew how come he wrote that Jew book about Benny Hurtz?"

Longarm laughed despite himself and replied, "I see you've never read the book. It does go on some. But the point of *Ben Hur*, once you wade on to the end, is how this right admirable gent of the Hebrew persuasion finds salvation and becomes one of the first Christians. I may be wrong, but I just can't see a serious Jew coming up with such a plot. I could be wrong, though—so what might anyone's religion have to do with the killings upstairs the other night?"

By this time the other guests, untended to by any of the siesta-bound Mex help, had gathered closer, some of the men dragging chairs from the other tables for the four women and their eight selves as the loudmouth who'd appointed himself their lawyer said, "Come on, you know New Mexico is run by that Jewish Santa Fe Ring, Deputy Long!"

Longarm answered, "No I don't. Governor Wallace was sent out this way to clean up the Santa Fe Ring, and my friends call me Custis."

The rude stranger extended his hand across the table

to declare that in that case *his* friends called him Dusty Wheeler.

Another male guest called Ballard got more to the point on how long the bunch of them figured to be confined to the posada grounds, spacious as they were. He said he'd come to Santa Fe to sell yard goods, not to laze by the river eating greaser grub off a steam table.

Longarm explained the peculiar hours of the posada staff and brought them more up-to-date on the string of mass murders punctuated by the one upstairs the other night. As he talked some and listened more betwixt bites of warmed-over grub, the pinned-down witnesses commenced to warm to him as he helped them understand, for the first time, what in the world they were doing there. For they'd been questioned back and forth and sideways by all sorts of lawmen who'd only informed them that *they* would ask the damned questions.

By the time Longarm was wiping his platter clean with a wad of tortilla, even Dusty Wheeler had relaxed some, and one of the women, the younger dark gal who'd been seated with the older one who'd told Longarm to watch his mouth, suggested they'd all feel more comfortable in the next-door lounge, which opened out onto a garden with a view of the river. So despite one gent's reservation about a southern exposure with high noon coming on, they went out, trusting Longarm's observation that they'd still be in the shade, with the sun at the zenith and any breezes headed their way having to cross cool running water and a flower garden. So they all helped themselves to more coffee and wandered over to the sure-enough more comfortable lounge to gather wicker furniture in a semicircle facing the flung-open windows overlooking what turned out to be an herb and kitchen garden, but you can't win 'em all.

Longarm didn't care. He figured he was ahead of the game. He'd been concerned that La Siesta, for all its vir-

51

tues in the dog days of August, was going to put everyone he wanted to talk to to bed until 3 P.M. at the earliest. But at Santa Fe's altitude La Siesta was more a matter of long-established custom than a pressing need, and so, whilst you couldn't find a Mex to jaw with by then, the out-of-town Anglos felt it was the middle of a balmy summer day and that nobody but yard dogs and lazy Mexicans ought to be lying down.

Longarm meant to question the posada staff later, in depth. But having just the guest list and the comfortable lounge to work with, he suspected he might get a less confused picture of the gunplay upstairs.

Assuming somebody wasn't lying like a rug, nobody there had even been aware of the high-stakes private card game down at the end of one hall.

The top floor of the sprawling posada was shaped like a big letter E, with two such gardens as they were gazing out on the river. The summer kitchen, stables and such connected to the main building had no second stories.

Dusty Wheeler, whom Longarm had suspected of tin-horn tendencies, had been surprised that a rambling sporting gent of his reputation hadn't been invited to the private game of the late Bustout Sosa. Wheeler said he'd heard tell of the high-stakes poker of the younger Anglo-Mex professional and come up from Lamy with intent to try his luck against the sassy kid.

Longarm was too kindhearted to point out the likely reasons a real high roller might not have wanted a tinhorn sitting in. He only observed that Dusty Wheeler had been lucky to be left out.

Ballard said, "I was reading about the same jasper pull-ing the same nasty stunt last month in Tombstone. Wouldn't those sporting gents killed here the other night have known how to read, and shouldn't they have been on the alert for trouble?"

Longarm said, "They likey were. As Frank and Jesse

52

discovered over to Northfield back in '76, even the spit-and-whistle crowd of a small town knows how to deal with trouble they're *expecting*. Gents of the sporting fraternity were doubtless aware of our unknown sore winner before any lawmen had connected a dotted line of similar crimes. So if there's one thing we know about whoever done it, he, she or it don't look like trouble until it's way too late. We figure it might have been a fake bellhop down to Tombstone. That ruse wouldn't have worked up here, because they were being served by a cantina waitress who's still alive and who gave a sworn deposition she left everybody else alive and playing poker the last time she delivered a tray of coffee upstairs."

"It's an inside job, engineered by International Jews," declared Dusty Wheeler, adding, "Everybody knows they're everywhere, working in cahoots on the sly. Aside from Lew the Jew, ain't the head of the BIA appointed by the same Jew president, a Jew named Karl Schmuck?"

Longarm gravely replied, "I believe Little Big Eyes, as the Indians call Secretary Schurz, was born a German Lutheran. At any rate he came to the States young, came out of the war a general and commenced to run for office on Republican tickets. This is the first time I've ever heard Little Big Eyes described as an International Jew."

"Then why did he appoint another Jew as his BIA agent to the Apache down by Fort Stanton?" Wheeler demanded.

Longarm started to speak before he considered, then nodded wearily and said, "If we are talking about the late Morris Bernstein of the Mescaler Agency, he was a property clerk, not the agent, hired before President Hayes appointed anybody anything out this way. Bernstein's murder was a federal offense, so I've read the transcripts."

That dark gal who'd suggested the move to the lounge asked what had happened to the unfortunate Bernstein.

Longarm said, "He was gunned down by a person or

persons unknown. The only witnesses were Mescalero wranglers, whose statements were taken with the usual pinch of salt. If they were telling it true, Morris Bernstein had been left alone and hence in charge when a gang of outlaws led by Billy the Kid or Dave Rudabaugh commenced to run off the agency remuda. Be it recorded Morris Bernstein took 'em on, single handed, and went down fighting like a man I'd be proud to drink with no matter how he might have said his prayers, if he said any prayers at all."

"Rudabaugh sounds like a Jew name," Wheeler replied thoughtfully.

Longarm snorted in disgust and replied, "It sounds as Dutch to me. As I recall his yellow sheets, old Dave—he's going on forty—was born in Missouri and raised on a Kansas farm, from whence he'd have gone to church, if he went to church at all, somewheres like that 'Little Brown Church in the Vale' they sing about."

Wheeler said he'd never heard tell of such a church.

Before Longarm could answer, that dark young gal threw her head back with a mocking smile to sing, right pretty . . .

"Oh come to the church in the wildwood,
Come to the church in the vale.
No place is as dear to my childhood,
As that little brown church in the vale!"

Longarm ticked his hat brim to her and allowed he couldn't have put it any clearer. He hadn't noticed how pretty she was until she'd sung so carefree. She was one of those petite and modestly dressed brunettes you could lose in a crowd if you didn't look close.

Once you had, of course, you could hardly help noticing how her half-grapefruit-sized cupcakes filled the bodice of her dark summer-weight but choke-collared dress.

He'd already established they had her down as Irene Glazer who'd come to teach school to Indian kids, along with that older Spanish-speaking Matilda Stern with way bigger tits but steel gray hair.

Since they hadn't sent him all that way to admire tits of any description, Longarm asked if they could leave the religious convictions of the killer or killers to one side for the moment as they tried to get a better picture of what might have happened up yonder.

A mousy little gal in a print summer frock ten years too young for her suddenly piped up, "Where's Jack of Diamonds? I'd forgotten all about him until Miss Glazer suddenly burst into song like that!"

The yard-goods-selling Ballard sat up straighter and exclaimed, "That's right! I'd clean forgot our Jack of Diamonds in all the confusion. I don't remember seeing him since that gunplay upstairs or . . . come to think of it, at suppertime earlier!"

So Longarm naturally asked who they might be talking about.

Ballard didn't look at Dusty Wheeler as he answered, "Tinhorn gambler by the looks of him. I think he signed in as Walters, or maybe Waters."

Irene Glazer said, "It was Walthers. He introduced himself to me without any encouragement on my part."

Longarm shook his head and said, "Nobody signed in out front by any such name. I've been over the transcripts, and nobody the law had down as a guest here seemes to be missing."

There came a buzz of disbelief. Irene said, "Surely you jest. He was here when we arrived two days ago. That evening, in this very lounge, he was the life of the party, or one of those pests who try to be."

Dusty Wheeler, of all folk, said, "Oh, I remember him. He wasn't sincere about gambling. It only took me a few questions to see he'd never really seen the elephant."

"Did he pronounce the H in Walthers?" asked Longarm, adding, "How come you all remember him as Jack of Diamonds?"

Ballard pointed at an upright piano against the 'dobe wall across the lounge and said, "He asked Miss Irene here to play it for him, and when she did, he sang it."

Irene rose to move over to the piano as she said, "Of course he had to pronounce the H in *Walthers*. How else would we have known it wasn't just plain *Walters*?"

As he followed her, Longarm explained, "You wouldn't have. *Walthers* with an H is the High Dutch spelling for *Walters*. It's pronounced *Walters* by them entitled by birthright to the name. So your Jack of Diamonds must have just helped himself to a name he read somewheres and pronounced it the way us Angry Saxons might."

Irene sat down at the upright, struck a chord and in that same pretty voice sang . . .

> "Jack of Diamonds, Jack of Diamonds,
> I know you of old.
> You've robbed my poor pockets of silver
>   and gold.
> So I'll eat when I'm hungry,
> And drink when I'm dry,
> And play Jack of Diamonds till the day that
>   I die!"

Ballard said, "That's just the way he sang it, almost as if he wanted us to remember him as a rambler and a gambler who played Jack of Diamonds . . . and then what?"

Longarm got out his notebook and a pencil stub as he quietly declared, "Then we agree on tightly detailed descriptions me and Santa Fe can put on wire as an all-points-want. For as I said before I got here, our best bet would be, and is, someone who was here around the time of that gunplay but made a run for it before we could check him out!"

Chapter 7

When it came siesta time, the staff of La Posada de San Francisco hadn't messed around. They'd left a small boy to watch over the tack room and stable, lest some untraditional *ladrónes* take unfair advantage of a long-established Spanish custom and try to steal things.

The bored kid was willing to try, but Longarm fetched his own bridle and saddle from the tack room and helped himself to the loan of a chestnut mare with white stockings.

When Longarm got to the Western Union he found, as he'd expected, that the nationwide telegraph company had somebody on duty twenty-four hours a damned day. The late Ezra Cornell hadn't died rich enough to endow his own university by running his Western Union according to the long-established Spanish custom of siesta.

After he'd alerted other lawmen far and wide to be on the lookout for a fleeing material witness or worse called Jack of Diamonds Walthers, Longarm scouted around the plaza in vain for any senior lawmen, Anglo or Mex, he'd be expected to consult on the matter.

There was nobody worth consulting. La Siesta was a custom easy to establish in the sort of dry sunny climates

Spanish-speaking folk tended to settle in. So he rode on back to the posada and tipped the kid for neither helping him nor hindering him as he put everything back where he'd found it.

He dropped by the steam table to gather another mug of coffee, and when he got back to the lounge he found it deserted, save for Irene Glazer, and she looked as if she surely wanted to be somewheres else.

As Longarm rejoined her, the petite brunette, who looked to be mayhaps French or of West Irish descent, told him everybody else had taken the advice of the Spanish-speaking Matilda Stern and repaired to their own quarters full of hot tamales, with nothing about to happen until for land's sake late in the afternoon.

Irene said, "Matilda explained La Siesta to me as we rode our train here from Topeka. She'd spent time in the Southwest before and I suspect she's picked up some lazy Mexican habits."

Longarm nodded and said, "It ain't hard, when habits make sense. I've heard tell the old-timey Spanish picked up the notion of La Siesta from them North African Moors they had so much truck with during the Middle Ages. Spain being high, sunny and dry as North Africa or say Mexico, old or new, the Moors and the Christian tribes they were feuding and fussing with when they weren't getting married up had just given up on trying to get a whole lot done under the blazing cloudless skies betwixt noon and, say, three or four when the sun ball stood low enough in the west to cast some tolerable shade outside."

Leaning back and sipping some cooled-off coffee, Longarm went on. "You'll discover after you've been out this way a spell that Mexicans ain't really all that lazy. They knock off work and shut things down in the middle of *our* day. But the business hours of Spanish-speaking folk ain't at all the same as ours. They open for beeswax before dawn and stay open past midnight over by the plaza. They put in the same twelve hours or so. They just prefer to be up and about when it ain't so blamed hot."

She stared at him thoughtfully and observed, "That's much the way Matilda explained things, albeit not in as tolerant a tone. Listening to the way she puts it, one might gather Mexicans are just quaint harmless folk one has to put up with. She just said she was going upstairs for a lie-down because there was nothing else to do with every-one else in town lying slug-a-bed. So tell me something, uh, Custis, just what denomination was that little church in the vale you went to?"

He shrugged and said, "My folk just called it going to church. Can't say they made a big deal of it. For a time, during the war, I felt sure there was nothing up there at all. It's easy to jump to conclusions when you're young and scared and disgusted."

"What faith do you follow now?" she murmured.

He shrugged and said, "Like that Jack of Diamonds eating when he's hungry and drinking when he's dry, I tend to go along with whatever might be offered at any weddings, funerals or such I'm invited to. The only thing I'm sure of is that I don't much cotton to anybody as sure of what's up there as the sky pilots who turn folk against one another in the name of their Merciful Lord, or what-ever they want to call it."

She dimpled and said, "*It?* Don't you mean *He?*"

He easily replied, "I call 'em as I see 'em. As I told this missionary one time, standing up for some Indian notions, it takes a bodacious self-confidence, in my opin-ion, to state with certainty you have any idea what the creator or first cause of all we see around us, out to the stars too far out to imagine, is really like or really aims to accomplish farther along."

Irene trilled the first few bars of "Farther Along," and one could have gotten the impression she'd spent a lot of time in Sunday school as a kid.

Then she cautiously asked, "Then you're an atheist, Custis?"

He said, "Not hardly. I outgrew that as I got older and wiser enough to see what a high opinion anyone would need to have of themselves to feel certain he or she knew how everything, out to the farthest stars, *got* there! Like I told that know-it-all missionary, the longer I ramble along the more comfortable I feel with the Lakota notion of Wakan Tonka."

"That would be the Great Spirit, right?" she asked brightly.

Longarm said, "That's how some missionaries have translated it. Wakan can be translated as *medicine, mystery, power* or *luck,* depending on how it's used. It adds up to a sort of big question mark in place of anything all that exact. A Contrary Society brave riding through the deadly field of fire from a Gatling gun, and making it, has Wakan. A chief you'd best pay attention to when he plans a hunt has Wakan. When something nobody understands just *happens,* that's Wakan too. In the case of Wakan Tonka it can be translated as *Big Medicine* or *Great Mystery* when you ask a medicine man what it's all about. Elders praying in a cloud of incense in a dark room can tell you how many feathers can be found on the average angel's wings. Others roaming across high plains under cloudless starry skies must not feel half as certain of who's pulling all the strings. If the Lakota had wanted to describe Wakan Tonka as *Great Spirit* they'd have said *Wanigi* Wanka. *Wanigi* is their word for spirit or spook."

She stared soberly at him as she said, "You don't sound as superior when you speak of Mexicans or Indians as Matilda does, and she has a degree in anthropology. You really don't care whether Governor Wallace might be Jewish or not, do you?"

Longarm sipped more joe and easily replied, "Why should I? Being brung up praying one way or another don't make you better or worse. As what you might best describe as an *observant lawman,* I have learned to judge folk by what they do, not how they pray. Had to shoot this one cuss who made the sign of the Cross every time he killed somebody. Arrested a Bible thumper in a clerical collar who shot Papists every chance he got, lest they breed and multiply. That Colonel Chivington who ordered Cheyenne children shot at Sand Creek was an ordained minister when he wasn't riding with the Third Colorado. That likely made him surer than me about who deserves to live or die in this uncertain world."

She looked away as she asked, "What about Jews? Have you had occasion to arrest many Jews out this way?"

He replied, "*Many* might be stretching things, but they do say Johnny Ringo might be of the Hebrew persuasion, and a handful of road agents on my wanted lists are Jewish for sure. Others would be Papist, Protestant or Buddhist, before you get to Mister Lo, the Poor Indian. They got more religions than we have, and once again the praying ain't as important as the *doing.* Even as we speak, Victorio, a Mission Papist, is off the reservation raising purely nasty hellfire and brimstone on both sides of the border as, meanwhile, his unreconstructed Navaho cousins are minding their own herds of sheep and not bothering a soul as they pray to Changing Woman."

He finished his mug and set it aside as he volunteered, "I sort of cotton to Changing Woman. She reminds me of that Chinee goddess of mercy, Miss Kuan Yin."

Irene blinked and marveled, "My lands, you respect the idols of the heathen Chinee as well?"

To which he could only reply, "Like that old hymn goes, 'Farther along we'll understand why.' Meanwhile who's to say I know as much about such stuff as your average Chinee? There's an awsome number of 'em, and they've been praying longer than most of us."

She laughed and said that reminded her of a silly joke

about Jews and Chinee. But when he asked her to tell it she looked away and said she wasn't sure how it went, not being Jewish.

He said in that case he'd have to ask Dusty Wheeler if *he* knew it, and that made her laugh so hard he feared she might fall out of her chair.

But she didn't, and as she calmed down she said, "I'm sorry. We have a name . . . I mean *they* have a name for . . . people like him."

Longarm volunteered, "The Mormons call 'em Gentiles."

She laughed less certainly and said, "Surely you jest? The Mormons are Christians of some sort, right?"

He nodded and said, "Church of Jesus Christ of Latter-Day Saints, as Mormon comes out in full, official. I asked one about that. He explained the word *Gentile* come down from the Latin for folk in general, or folk who ain't like *us,* whoever *we* may be."

Irene said she'd heard the Mormons had had almost as much trouble as the Jews out West. Longarm said, "Way more. Fools like Dusty Wheeler will go on about Jewish plots to take over the country, if not the world, but many a gent of the Hebrew persuasion has managed to prosper out this way. They may not like him, they may poke fun at his whiskers and ways, but nobody ever threw old Meyer Guggenheim and his brother out a window just for being a copper baron."

"What about that boy at the Mescalero Agency, Bernstein?"

"He was killed by horse thieves more interested in agency horseflesh than in his religion," Longarm answered.

She sighed and said, "Just the same, I wonder if they would have killed him if he'd changed his name for business reasons and, you know, sort of went along with the way things are out here."

Longarm doubted she wanted to be asked if she was by any chance related to old Aaron Glassmann who sold and repaired guns down Denver way. So he shrugged and said, "Can't say what I might do in that position. As you all saw earlier, that Jew-baiting tinhorn Wheeler called me a Jew boy after I'd introduced myself by my Angry Saxon name."

"That's funny, you don't look Jewish." She dimpled with a Mona Lisa smile and added, "I wonder what made him take you for Jewish."

Longarm answered without hesitation, "Spite. He didn't like me because I reminded him of how little he saw when he looked in the mirror, I reckon. After that, not liking Jewish folk for whatever reason, he decided I ought be one. Back in Salem Village that time, another gaggle of spiteful geese decided to go hunting for witches. When they couldn't find any witches, for the simple reason there was no such thing, they murdered a whole bunch of their less popular neighbors as close enough."

Irene looked away and murmured, "There's this old Russian saying that goes, 'When you see a Jew, beat him. He will know why.'"

"Are you Russian, Miss Irene?" he asked before he'd had time to think.

She said, "My grandparents came from there. My parents were born in New York City and I was born upstate in a place called Lockport. I don't think you'll find many other . . . Russians in Lockport. *Shlim genug*—I mean, bad enough you should be *Irish* in Upstate New York!"

He nodded and said, "Same deal. I remember this sign in a shop window in this Eastern town we were marching through. It said they wanted help but no Irish need apply. You'd think such a welcome to a new land might inspire some serious thought. But during them riots out Frisco way, Dennis Kearny posted banners reading that since they were running all the heathen Chinee out of the country they ought to finish off the Christ killers. No man who runs his brain on hate can be expected to keep it on the tracks and—Hold on! You're the second lady in as many days who's inspired *my* brain to consider how many folk out this way might be acting as something they ain't!"

"What are you suggesting I might really be?" she blazed.

He soothed, "There ain't that much mystery about *you,* Miss Irene. You say you and Miss Matilda have been hired out this way to teach Indian kids, and that would be duck-soup simple to check out if I had any call to doubt you. I'm talking about somebody acting *serious* to his true identity, and as you just now inspired me to wonder, the *reasons* for so much deadly spite. There's all sort of ways to rob a man without killing him. Our Mister Jack of Diamonds has to be twisted up inside, like that pathetic tinhorn Dusty Wheeler. He must have some reason, or think he has some reason, for busting in and blowing everybody away like that."

She suggested, "Dead men tell no tales? Leave no witnesses to describe you to the law?"

Then she added with an intelligent frown, "Are you sure the mystery man we knew only as Jack of Diamonds Walther with an H is the one you want, Custis?"

He said, "Not hardly. It's the possible name I just put out on the wire. It's about time we had *something* to call him. After that it makes you sort of wonder what a man who wasn't really staying here as a guest was doing in this very lounge, leaving a name and description he never had to before he or *somebody* pulled something mighty spooky on poor old Bustout Sosa and his fellow poker players!"

She repressed a yawn and said, "If you say so. This is all too much for me to fathom." Then she yawned again and said, "My lands, Matilda was right. These lazy Mex customs seem to be catching, and you say there's not a thing we can do about our Jack of Diamonds until after three?"

When he allowed that was about the size of it, she rose to her feet to announce, "In that case I may as well toddle on up to my room, and if I can't catch forty winks, perhaps a change into a fresher dress before it comes time to rejoin the human race may perk me up a bit."

He said, "Lots of ladies take sponge baths during their siestas, or so I hear tell."

She agreed that seemed a swell suggestion and had made it all the way to the archway before she noticed he was just sitting there, lighting a smoke, and quietly asked, "Well, aren't you coming?"

To which Longarm could only reply as he sprang to his feet and got rid of the fool smoke, "Not yet, Miss Irene. But if you're offering, I sure would like to!"

Chapter 8

He'd said that in a joshing tone, of course, and she'd sounded just as skylarking when she replied she'd been afraid he'd never ask. So they both were laughing as they went up the stairs together, and they both knew nobody was supposed to mean it as they talked sassy back and forth down the hall as far as her room, which came before his. So when they stopped there, all Longarm could come up with was "Well, here we are."

To which Irene replied with a giggle, "Well, won't you come in? I don't seem half as sleepy up here as I did down there."

So he followed her in and shut and barred the hall door after him, and as he turned around Irene was already "making myself more comfortable."

The next thing they knew they were at it like old pals. She came with a groan they must have been able to hear for a furlong and then asked in a dumbfounded tone, "What are we *doing* at this hour, Custis? It can't be two in the afternoon and I thought we were tallking religion and . . . Oh, do it some *more,* you sneaky horrid thing!"

So he did, without comment. Old Abe Randall had warned him there'd be gals like this. The older soldier had advised that when in the company of gals who felt they had to say *something* it was best to just let them have their say. She wasn't really talking to him as she dug her nails into his butt and tried to swallow him alive with her old ring-dang-doo. She was out to convince herself none of what was going on was her fault and that he must have taken her proper platonic invite all wrong, Lord love him.

When she wanted to get on top he thought it was a swell notion, because she was such a tiny little thing a man could buy her notion that he was taking cruel advantage of her if she hadn't been doing most of the work as she sort of milked his maypole with mighty inspired gyrations. She never said it, but he suspected she hadn't been getting any lately after a much more active love life back East. He knew that if he asked her she'd tell him all about the wicked men who'd used and abused her weak warm nature. So he never asked.

With her on top, by broad daylight he could see she might be a tad older than she let on, although her trim nude torso was as yet unmarred by Time's cruel teeth. She simply looked more . . . grown-up as she took charge in the well-versed way only a gal who'd been married up or had worked as a whore a spell could ever seem to manage.

That was the trouble with the unfair quest of most men for a virgin pure who'd screw you bowlegged the first time you could get her alone. Knowing most gals were searching for a Mister Right who'd been saving all his hard-ons for them and them alone, he was glad she was content to compliment him for the way he managed to include her clit without asking him where he'd ever learned that trick.

As he'd shut and barred the hall door, Longarm had taken another door set in the side wall of Irene's room for a closet, but he hadn't cared; his duds and Irene's dress weren't going anywhere as their owners went at it naked as jays. He'd naturally hung his six-gun on a bedpost, but figured everything else could go on the floor, to be gathered up when and if anybody ever needed them again.

Hence, having lost track of that one oaken door in the 'dobe side wall, he was startled considerable when it suddenly popped open and a familiar voice let fly with, "What's wrong, Irene? Are you all right? Oh . . . bless my soul, I'm sorry!"

As the matronly Matilda Stern crawfished backwards to slam the door after her, Longarm felt no call to ask Irene why she hadn't warned him she and her older pal had checked into adjoining rooms that shared a damned door. He'd already noticed she was sort of impulsive.

As if to prove it, Irene laughed like hell, bouncing up and down, then sort of sobbed, "Oh, my God, I don't know how I'll ever explain this to poor Matilda!"

He suggested, "Why explain it? She surely knows what she just now saw with her own eyes."

She dithered, "I'd better talk to her. You'd better go. After we come again, I mean!"

So he rolled her over onto her naked back to finish faster with an elbow hooked under either little shapely knee and her legs as wide open as they'd go without doing permanent damage. He couldn't tell if she was begging him to stop or to do it faster in some outlandish old-country lingo until he shot his wad for sure and she gasped, *"Oy veh ist mir!* I may convert!"

Then she commenced to cry and beg him to get off her. So he did, and a few minutes later he was back in his own room, going over the transcripts of those earlier bust-ins of Jack of Diamonds.

Longarm knew better, but try as he might, he couldn't help thinking of the still unknown killer as Jack of Diamonds Walthers with an H, now that Irene and those others had offered the law a handle to grab hold of. But that still left them with a slippery son of a bitch who just didn't seem to think like other human beings. Unless other human beings were dead wrong about the few sure facts they thought they had to work with.

The inexact number of nationwide killings had some few facts in common to make them look like the work of the same killer or killers. In every case the victims had numbered no more than a dozen and no fewer than five high rollers engaged in an invitation-only game of high-stakes poker. The exact form of poker had varied some, but that hardly mattered when you considered that any game of high-stakes poker would by definition require some serious money to be on hand. Other varieties of card games were *gambling,* and you only won regular at gambling by cheating. The sort of jaspers who played high-stakes poker were inclined to be more respectable, as well as richer, than tinhorns such as Dusty Wheeler. Tinhorns such as Dusty Wheeler weren't invited and seldom knew about such private games.

So how might a self-confessed tinhorn of the ilk of Jack of Diamonds worm his way within point-blank pistol range of elite sporting gents on the prod for trouble?

He'd surely never have gone upstairs and banged on the door after entertaining all those other guests by—he wasn't a guest. He'd never checked in down at the desk. He'd just wandered in out of the night to join folk in the lounge who'd had no call to question his being there.

The gunplay upstairs lay a night in the future. *How come* it had lain a full night in the future? As he read over that part of the transcripts again, Longarm saw that Jack of Diamonds had gone into his song and dance before any of the high rollers fated to die upstairs were on the premises.

"But the organizer, Bustout Sosa, had no doubt already sent out his invitations, with payday coming up!" Longarm murmured aloud.

So what if the gent calling himself Walthers with an

70

H and managing to be remembered as Jack of Diamonds *wanted it known* he'd been there the night *before* the gunplay upstairs and just as surely *hadn't* been there the night the high rollers who'd never invited him to play got wiped out and robbed?

"That makes no sense!" Longarm informed a thoughtful smoke ring as it drifted teasingly away. He added, "If Jack of Diamonds wanted it known he wasn't here the night of the robbery, all he'd have had to do was stay the hell away, right?"

He consulted his watch. He saw things might be coming to life around the plaza by the time he got there, if he just strolled over on foot. It wasn't all that far, and sitting still with ants running 'round in your skull could hurt way worse.

As he followed his lengthening shadow up Cathedral Road, Longarm knew it was still too blamed hot in Santa Fe. But once he made it to the rustic shade of the governor's palace—or palace of the governors, as it came out in Spanish—others were out and about, and it didn't take him long to scout up Marshal Harris. He knew once he got the go-ahead from old Iggy there'd be no need to go hat in hand to other local lawmen.

It was still stuffy inside. So they enjoyed a set-down with *cerveza* under the overhang of a sidewalk cantina over in Burro Alley where the sun never shone enough for the 'dobe walls to hold the heat.

Marshal Harris was pleased to hear about Jack of Diamonds and agreed it was time they give the son of a bitch a name, even if it wasn't his and he hadn't done it. Like Longarm, the local lawman couldn't see any sensible point to a gent who wasn't registered at the posada, wasn't known at the posada and hadn't done anything sensible at the posada working so hard to be *remembered* at the posada.

Longarm said, "Could have been what stage magicians

call *misdirection*. What makes you so sure Jack of Diamonds wasn't known to the regular staff over yonder?"

Harris said, "We asked if anyone from around town had been by within suspicion time of the gunplay. They helped us establish that none of their guests that night were Santa Fe folk. Santa Fe folk would have no call to check into transient quarters. But Santa Fe folk who were up to something might. What does *misdirection* mean?"

Longarm said, "This stage-magic gal I met up on the north range a spell back explained how a magician aiming to pull a rabbit out of his hat might show you the hat was empty, then get you to look at something else whilst his assistant stuffed a rabbit in the hat. She said sometimes they can get away with that in plain view of the audience because said audience is all goggle-eyed at something else taking place on the same stage."

Harris said, "I've often wondered how they do that hat trick. What do you reckon they were stuffing into what whilst they had everybody watching Jack of Diamonds down in the lounge?"

Longarm said, "Don't know. According to the depositions I've been reading, none of the hired help spread all over the posada saw anything that struck 'em as unusual during, before or after the sudden burst of gunfire up in Sosa's hired room at one end of the corridor."

Harris grimaced and said, "That's about the size of it. Down Tombstone way the killer or killers may have somehow gotten through the door as a part of room service nobody had ordered. This time the few trays that were taken up from the late night cantina went in and out uneventful. In sum, one minute they were playing high-stakes poker behind a locked door and the next minute they all lay dead on the floor with all their money gone."

Longarm said, "I read nothing about shotgun blasts this time. Did your county coroner probe for birdshot as well as .41 slugs?"

Harris shrugged and said, "I reckon. He'd have reported it had they found anything all that unusual. Try her this way: There weren't as many to cover with that fowling piece, so they never brought one. They just got in some mighty sudden sneaky way and had everybody dead on the floor before they knew what hit them."

Longarm said, "That's surely what it looks like, and I can't make it work. We've both made arrests at gunpoint. Can you see covering more'n two or three men at a time? A man with sand in his draw can draw and fire with a bullet in his heart. That's how come so many gunfights end up with both parties dead on the ground. Man with a bullet in his heart sure feels poorly, but it takes a spell for his brain to die. I read how this French doctor has been 'spearminting with the heads of the recently guillotined. Don't ask me how he figured this out, but he's sure some chopped-off heads live as long as thirty seconds, for all the good it does 'em. A man with a lot more still connected could put up a hell of a fight in thirty seconds."

The amiable but firm-jawed Anglo-Mex said, "I've shot more than one man in the heart and they just fell down."

Longarm nodded and said, "Lucky for us, most do. But consider how *many* armed and dangerous victims Jack of Diamonds has had to take out, and then consider how fucked up things could go if only *one* of them managed thirty seconds of wit and guts."

Harris shrugged and said, "It could happen. It ain't. And Jack of Diamonds may not have read about them guillotine 'spearmints. I know *I* haven't."

Then he brightened and asked, "Wouldn't it be a pisser and save us lots of trouble if the next time the sneaky cocksucker shoots somebody the cuss just grits his teeth and shoots back?"

"We'd have a real locked-room mystery then." Longarm smiled before he added, "I'd like to turn those guests at the posada loose, Marshal. We can't hold anybody longer than seventy-two hours on suspicion alone, and you've already heard my arguments for not holding folk we don't have any call to suspect."

The marshal said, "I suspect everybody until they're proven innocent. Ain't you ever heard of the Spanish Inquisition?"

Then he grinned and said, "Let's cut 'em loose and see what happens. I got no call to pester the governor or the county sheriff about the move. Do you?"

Longarm agreed the one they had to question serious was the mysterious Jack of Diamonds, even though he wasn't sure what he wanted to accuse the son of a bitch of.

They finished their Mex beer and parted friendly, with Harris heading back to open his office and Longarm legging it back to the posada, as it seemed to be getting even cooler.

And so was the case, he'd decided by the time he got back to find all the others gathered in the lounge, with the staff members up and serving them as if making up for the three-hour siesta.

Longarm knew they weren't. They'd be as willing to serve at midnight, and felt no guilt at all about what they might or might not have been doing in their quarters all that time.

Longarm told the assembled witnesses who didn't seem to know anything that they were free to stay or go as long as none of them left the Santa Fe area without good reason, and related it to the law before they left.

Dusty Wheeler wanted to know just how much leeway that word *area* gave a man. Longarm said, "Let's agree on east of the Upper Rio Grande and west of the Sangre de Cristos, no farther south than Cerrillos or north of Cundiyo."

Looking as if butter wouldn't melt in her mouth, Irene

Glazer piped up, "The Sangre de Cristos are those red rock peaks you can see from my window upstairs, right?"

Longarm nodded and said, "Name means Blood of Christ. If you look at 'em from your window at sundown against a darkening sky you'll see why."

Before Irene could answer, her older chum, Matilda Stern, snapped, "We shan't be here at sunset. Since we're no longer being held here we'll be going on to our mission school now!"

Most of the others there agreed it was time to be moving on. Longarm let them sort it out as he ambled back to the lobby entrance to scout up some of the Mex hired help.

The older man at the desk—he said he was a Pablo Montoya—looked as if he was fixing to cry as he told Longarm, "I knew you wish for to speak with all of us. I told them all not to go anywhere else before you spoke to them. But Gertruda, she is not here. Nobody can tell me where she is!"

Longarm started to go for his notebook, thought harder, then asked if they were talking about the waitress who'd been running trays in and out of that fatal poker game upstairs.

Montoya said, "*Sí,* that is for why I am so upset. You needed to talk to her about the mystery, no?"

Longarm smiled thinly as he decided, "Ain't certain things are half as mysterious now."

Chapter 9

Up at his officious federal office off the plaza, Marshal Harris said the missing Gertrudo Moreno only read two ways to him: She'd lit out on her own or somebody had lit her out. In either case she added up to part of a much less mysterious inside job.

Seated across the marshal's desk from him, nursing a tequila in a visitor's chair way more comfortable than the one Billy Vail provided, Longarm flicked some ash in the swell copper ashtray stand in the 'dobe-walled but hospitable office and said, "Our Jack of Diamonds used her, somehow, to help him get the drop on Bustout Sosa and his private poker game. Going back over the inexact records we have on what seems the same murderous son of a bitch, it ain't obvious until you double-check, but in many a case one or more members of the hotel staff has wound up missing or worse at the time or shortly after somebody called the law."

Harris nodded and said, "He started out modest, pulling his stunt a good two or three months apart. Then, when nobody *caught* the cocksucker, he started hitting once a month, and this last time just a week after he left Tombstone with twenty grand or more. What do you suppose he does with all that money?"

Longarm blew a thoughtful smoke ring and said, "I'll ask him when we catch him. Living expenses are considerable along the Owlhoot Trail, and if we're talking about a gang instead of one master criminal . . . See what I mean? He, she, it or them still has us flimflammed. All this angle on the likely late Gertruda Moreno gives us is an educated guess about the way they move in. Just barging in behind a waiter or waitress won't work for me. Picture your ownself seated on the far side of a card table with a gun on your hip or in its shoulder holster when the whole damned James and Younger gang comes in at you behind a flying coffee tray. Do you aim to sit there like a big-ass bird or for Gawd's sake *try* for your own gun?"

Harris nodded soberly and said, "We've considered pushing our luck after more than one killer had everybody covered with their hands up."

"And their guns still on 'em?" Longarm dryly asked.

The local marshal frowned thoughtfully and said, "I follow your drift. Men will go along with their own cold-blooded executions to a point. Line half a dozen men in front of a firing squad, wearing their guns with their hands untied, and a neat and tidy one-sized execution can get problematic!"

"We're still missing something. I suspect Gertruda Moreno was in on it and somebody didn't want her to tell us about it. That part don't worry me as much as what in blue blazes Gertruda *did* for Jack of Diamonds or whoever."

Harris started to suggest something dumb. But then he nodded and said, "You're right. It had to be something slicker than just knocking on the door for the Big Bad Wolf. I've been studying on what you said before about misdirection. That uninvited sing-along staged by Jack of Diamonds in that posada lounge *must* have been meant to puzzle the shit out of this child, because it has. Try as I might, I can't come up with a sensible reason a crook planning a murderous robbery would show up ahead of time to show everybody what he looked like!"

Longarm said, "Neither can I. So my best bet may be to just ask him, once I catch up with him."

Harris asked, "How do you figure on that, old son? Billy Vail tells me you're good—but tracking down a man you've never seen in a town the size of Santa Fe?"

Longarm said, "Old Billy Vail calls what I'll be up to the process of eliminating. It was invented by this old-time English sage back in the 1300s. His name was William of Ockham, and some call it Ockham's Razor. You start with the whole ball of wax and then you commence to shave away, or eliminate, until the next thing you know what's left looks like the only answer."

He took a deep drag, snorted it out and continued, "For example, here in Santa Fe County, many if not most grown men are of Hispanic persuasion, no offense. So we can eliminate more than half the suspects right off. He might or might not have been a local resident. If he's known around Santa Fe, he ought to be known as a flashy tinhorn given to breaking into song about the Jack of Diamonds."

"Unless that was an act designed to have us *look* for a flashy tinhorn given to singing Jack of Diamonds," the senior lawman who knew the place better pointed out, adding, "I'm paid to keep an eye on such gents. The last time the quick-draw artist Jim Dolan drew up a chair in the back room of the Trail's End Saloon, I knew about it before the game was over."

Longarm grimaced and observed, "Needless to say, you never heard of any cheerfully singing tinhorn answering to the descriptions offered by all them other strangers to Santa Fe. So our Jack of Diamonds is a recent addition to your sporting scene, or a local boy making bad who put on a big flashy act in order to ... You're right, and I just hate to chase my own tail like a blood-hound puppy!"

He dug out his notebook and read off, "Average-built Anglo with a brown mustache and lighter hair under a brown new-looking Boss model Stetson with a Texas creased crown. Flashy vest of chocolate silk brocade with gold stitching and likely fake diamond buttons. Pongee summer suit. Pongee—that's raw rope-colored Chinee silk, spun from gathered wild kin to the domesticated silk-worm."

Harris looked disgusted and said, "I know what a pon-gee summer suit looks like. They sell 'em over to the Gomez Emporium, and lots of gents in these parts buy 'em when it commences to heat up."

"With brown ten-gallon hats and diamond-studded bro-cade vests?" Longarm interjected, going on to say, "After that, Dusty Wheeler, a professional gambler, opined Jack of Diamonds wasn't half as smart about cards as he let on. Said he made more than one slip that evening as he bragged about playing Jack of Diamonds all over creation, and I didn't need to have old Dusty tell me that song ain't one he made up for the occasion. Sort of reminds me of *Deadwood Dick*."

"*Deadwood Dick*'s a song?" asked the marshal, who'd been out West all his life, making him a rare Westerner.

Longarm said, "*Deadwood Dick* began as a penny dreadful magazine put out in London, England. The yarns were written by an Englishman who'd never been to the States, let alone the West, but thought *Deadwood* sounded American enough for his hero, an American detective called Deadwood Dick."

"I can't say I ever read about that Deadwood Dick," said Harris.

Longarm said, "Others must have. Aside from plagia-rized dime novels written by American hack writers, there were at last count three whole Deadwood Dicks, in the flesh and signing autographs from the Black Hills east and west. One's a befuddled English drunk who may have read the original stories before he found himself prospecting in vain near Deadwood, Dakota Territory, and seeing his name was Richard, commenced to prospect for drinking money by autographing postcards from Deadwood."

"You mean he made himself up. Can you do that?" Harris laughed.

Longarm chuckled and asked, "Why not? Didn't Calamity Jane convince a whole lot of reporters to buy drinks for her by claiming to be the one true love of James Butler Hickok, who was happily married at the time of his death to the younger and way prettier Augusta Lake of bareback-riding fame? The next most famous Deadwood Dick, in dark towns along the railroad tracks east of the Mississippi, would be a gentleman of color named Nate—not Richard—Love. Sells autographed sepia tones of himself gussied up as a cowhand in batwing chaps. May have worked as a cowhand in his day. Tells a mighty odd tale of how he got to be Deadwood Dick, riding for prizes in a Deadwood stock show back in '76 and winning every event."

Harris asked, "Would they have been holding a stock show in a mining camp just getting built in 1876?"

Longarm shrugged and said, "They didn't even have Calamity Jane yet. She showed up after her Wild Bill had been dead and buried by his wife a spell before she let it be known Wild Bill was her one true love and the father of her six-year-old love child, Jean Hickok, albeit not one reporter to date has ever managed to put the two of them in the same barroom whilst Hickok was alive."

"You mean he never even knew her?" marveled Harris.

Longarm shrugged and said, "Might have had her pointed out to him along the way as a peril to be avoided despite her willing ways. Some say they call her *Calamity* because she has every known social disease, and body lice as well. But I dunno, she's still alive, and I digressed from the Deadwood Dicks of this land."

"There's more?" said the Southwesterner, laughing.

Longarm said, "Last one I met was just a plain old trash-white American barfly, with no postcards to sell but a better story. He says he was the inspiration for the Deadwood Dick of the limey penny dreadfuls because he tried to sell them his autobiography and they stole the plot after saying it was too wild for their readers."

Marshal Harris decided, "In sum, you and Mister Ockham figure Jack of Diamonds is just a borrowed handle and we have to keep an open mind as we scout for a flashy gent who may or may not have on the same outfit."

Longarm snorted, "Me and old Bill Ockham are just getting started, for Pete's sake. Assuming he was in on it, he may have gone to ground with his share of the loot. I say *assuming* he was in on it because we've yet to decide on him as we brandish the razor. He was there, acting suspicious, but so was Dusty Wheeler, and nobody, so far, can place either one of them in that private poker game that turned out so ugly."

"He was there to draw attention away from something or somebody else," opined Harris.

Longarm replied he'd just said that and opined they were talking in circles. So they shook on that and parted friendly so's Longarm could do some serious saloon scouting as the shadows grew ever longer.

There was a heap of saloons to choose from as Santa Fe recovered from its lazy afternoon nap. The founding Spanish colonials had not been the gold-gaga conquistadors who'd explored the shit out of the Southwest and gone home empty-handed after reporting that all those Indian yarns about golden cities were *mierda del toro*. By sheet-shithouse misfortune the Spanish who were there first never noticed all the gold, silver and copper lodes north of Old Mexico before they lost them all in that Mexican War. So Santa Fe and Spanish settlements like it, all the way out to Frisco Town, had been settled sort of the way the ancient Romans had colonized their world, with solid construction on sensible town sites meant to last. You didn't find Western ghost towns built Spanish style. But if they lacked the bust of Anglo mushroom towns, they lacked the boom as well. There wouldn't have been much to inspire an Anglo territorial capital within miles of Santa Fe if there hadn't been such a swell town already handy when the Anglos took over. As their short-line Santa Fe Southern intimated, Santa Fe was too out of the way to grow into a railroad town like Cheyenne or a railroad and meat-packing town like Omaha. There'd been no gold strike like the one in Denver's Cherry Creek to inspire all those 'dobe walls and red tile roofs, and anybody who studied Wall Street much could see that towns such as Deadwood, Tombstone or even Virginia City were not as long for this world as Santa Fe.

Santa Fe had commenced as a mission to the poor heathen Indians, no matter what they wanted to be. There'd been times, early on, the local Indians had put up a hell of a fight. They said that back in 1680 the Indians rose under a San Juan pueblo leader called Popé whose conversion hadn't taken. Fanning out from the big Tanoan pueblo of Taos, the Indians had chased the Spanish missionaries and the garrison meant to protect them down the Rio Grande to Old Mexico. So when they'd come back with a bigger garrison twelve years later, they got things right, under a regular Spanish government, one hell of a lot of *soldados* and all the dependents it took to keep the capital of a Spanish colony running *right*. The farms and stock spreads all around were there to feed the government center. It was mostly a government town in a sparsely settled territory. So Santa Fe attracted what might

82

best be described as carpetbaggers rather than the mining and beef barons you found in other Western towns of the same size.

This had resulted in recent Wild West doings that reporters, used to the range wars and claim jumpings in other parts, had a hard time describing.

There was more open range in New Mexico than any outfit could hope to graze, let alone fight over. The reporters seemed to think skinny-ass kid cattle thieves were behind all the recent gunplay out New Mexico way. But the most dangerous men in New Mexico were the political hacks out to horn in on the government contracts and such, which could be milked for cash in a territory where government was still about the only game in town.

All that bullshit even Western papers had carried about the so-called Lincoln County War had described it as a range war, when it had been no such thing. Grown-up, respectable-looking men who hired gun waddies to back their grabs for government beef contracts were the ones Longarm would have hung had it been up to him. But it wasn't, and they hadn't sent him all that way to help Lew Wallace tidy up the wolf-pack politics of New Mexico.

So he drifted hither and drifted yon as he followed the brighter lights and louder piano-roll music of a town that stayed wide open after midnight. He made no bones about who he was or who he might be looking for. He sat in at more than one friendly little game, losing less than he won without making anybody sore, the way a good poker player wanted things to go. Playing cards or bellied to the bar with a cross section of Santa Fe night life, Anglo, Mex, male and she-male, Longarm wasn't able to get a line on any tinhorn they knew who answered the description of Jack of Diamonds. But he figured that might be something worth slicing away with Ockham's Razor. If nobody like Jack of Diamonds was known around Santa Fe, he was new in town, or *local* gussied up *unusual*.

New in town worked better when you considered the killings in Tombstone and other parts. It hardly seemed likely those high rollers in Tombstone had been murdered and robbed by a local bad man waiting there for them.

The killings had occurred over a long period, on both sides of the Big Muddy, before he, she, it or they had made the mistake with that federal want and those BIA funds. So some damned body had to be riding the Owlhoot Trail from town to town, hitting high-stakes games that had been meant to be private.

That was something to think about. But wondering how a stranger in town might hear of a private high-stakes game didn't carry him all that farther along Jack of Diamond's trail.

So at about 1 A.M., having drawn nothing but blanks and a whole lot of draft beer, Longarm was ready to pack it in, and would have, if he hadn't noticed a commotion over by the Sheriff's Department and strode over to see what could be up at that hour.

A county lawman who'd been at the meeting with the governor called out to him as he approached, "Ask our wrangler out back to outfit you with some hooves if you'd care to ride with us for Cerrillos, Uncle Sam!"

Longarm said, "Well, sure I'll come for you by moonlight, but where might we be going?"

The county man replied, "Cerrillos, where the Tucson Trail crosses the railroad tracks west of Lamy. One of them suspects we were watching over to that posada must have wanted to catch a train. He got into it with a Mex he called a Jew boy and now he's dead, and the Mex who gunned him is still at large!"

Chapter 10

By the time they'd outfitted Longarm with a cordovan barb and a center-fire, dally-roping saddle with an early Winchester Yellow Boy, he had to lope some to overtake the posse as it dusted up the moonlight at a not too comfortable mile-eating trot down the Tucson Trail.

Like the Bozeman Trail, the Chisholm Trail and of course the Santa Fe Trail, the Tucson Trail had been overtaken by a changing West and no longer made her half as far as Tucson through Indian country served by the Iron Horse. But it would get you down to Cerrillos if you followed it south-southwest for a good forty miles.

It would have taken them over twenty-four hours to make it on the mounts they'd started out on, of course. But there was no Santa Fe Southern line down to that railroading town, and so a stage line served travelers along that route, and where there was a stage line there were stage stops every ten or twelve miles where a stagecoach, or a sheriff's posse, could swap to fresh horses and maintain a nine-or-ten-mile-an-hour average, because your average mount could trot at that speed for an hour before it was all trotted out for a spell.

Taking advantage of the way stations, they rode into

Cerrillos around cock's crow, to find the undersheriff and his deputies down that way not only up but anxious to see them.

The four hours and change in the saddle had given Longarm time for some mental arithmetic. So he knew that although there'd been no way Dusty Wheeler had dragooned stage line mounts for his own use, he'd managed to get there before midnight, leaving Santa Fe earlier than three-thirty or four in the afternoon. It only worked one way: He'd come down by stage.

But Longarm wasn't in command, nobody liked a know-it-all and he had a lathered mount to tend to—in this case a gelding of the chestnut saddle breed the army remount service favored and sold off cheap after they were eight years old, in about the shape of a thirty-year-old athlete with a half dozen years of stage hauling left in him, or her.

Longarm helped the possemen delegated the task to lead the borrowed mounts around to the stage line's paddock to unsaddle 'em, water 'em and rub 'em down with the help of the Mex station crew. By they time they were able to join the county gold badges in the local deputy coroner cum horse doctor's carriage house–morgue, the senior deputy he'd ridden down with had secured depositions from the eager-to-help local townees who'd seen the shoot-out around 10 P.M. the night before. So old Dusty Wheeler, so cold, so dead and so bare on the zinc-topped examining table, had for sure lit out by stage as soon as he was able and must have gotten into it down this way right after he arrived.

The county man Longarm had come down with nodded at the now stiff tinhorn with what looked like shirt buttons of scab down his shirtless front as he said, "The way most saw it, the late Dusty Wheeler transacted some beeswax over to the railroad yards, sauntered into the Tuna Blossom Saloon and called a Mex at the bar a sneaky fucking

Jew boy before all hell busted loose. They say Wheeler might have winged the Mex. You know how it gets in a saloon fight, with all that smoke swirling 'round. Some who were closer think they saw the Mex whirl twice around and totter for the door as they were losing track of him in the smoke. Time the smoke cleared he was long gone. But the same could not be said for the man who'd called him a Jew boy and slapped leather on him. Mex must have been packing double action to climb Wheeler's frame like that. Witnesses said the Mex didn't look all that Jewish to them. Why do you reckon he called him a Jew boy?"

Longarm grimaced and replied, "Old Dusty was like that. Anybody he didn't cotton to had to be part of that International Conspiracy of the Elders of Zion. They said it looked as if the two of them acted as if they knew one another?"

The county law said, "The gist of their brief conversation, as recalled by the barkeep, has Wheeler saying something like 'What are you doing down here? What's your game, you sneaky fucking Jew boy?' Nobody remembers the Mex saying shit. There are times to flap your mouth and there are times to slap leather. So Wheeler wound up dead and the Mex got away. Might have got away clean aboard a D&RG night train that stopped here in the wee small hours. I aim to wire the Texas Rangers in El Paso to watch for a *sangre-azul* wearing an expensive silver-mounted charro outfit and a sombrero of the same color with silver braid. He might be wounded. He's likely to be packing a double-action Colt .38, like they say Billy the Kid packs."

Longarm suggested, "Whilst you're at it, have the rangers keep an eye peeled for a likely prosperous-looking mestiza called Gertruda Moreno. Ain't all that many mestiza gals getting off Pullman cars, and if she was in on it she'd be traveling first class these days."

The local undersheriff, who'd been talking to the deputy coroner, came over in time to catch some of Longarm's drift. He said, "Gertruda Moreno, you say? What's she done now?"

Longarm said, "I mean to ask her. You say you know her?"

The local undersheriff said, "Watched her grow up. Her folk raise pigs and chickens down the tracks a piece. They're all right, I reckon, but little Gertruda is something else. Pretty as a picture and stubborn as a mule, with no head for figures or right from wrong. Last I heard of her she was working as a whore up Santa Fe way."

Longarm looked at the senior deputy he'd ridden down with. The Santa Fe lawman nodded and said, "I had her down in *my* notebook as a waitress. What if she volunteered for a lower-paying job just to wind up where she wound up that night, sashaying in and out of that high-stakes game?"

Longarm said, "She may or may not have come down by coach with that Mex Wheeler called a Jew boy with fatal results. Neither could have come down on the late coach with Wheeler, or some confrontation would have happened earlier. So let's say the Mex couple caught the morning coach and Wheeler caught the afternoon coach. That works for me."

The undersheriff asked, "How do you know Gertruda rode down with that cuss in the braided sombrero? She ain't the sort of gal who needs an escort to get about, you know."

Longarm explained, "Add it up. She came down from Santa Fe. He must have come down from Santa Fe if Wheeler knew him, and from the way Wheeler called the Mex he must have known him from up yonder and suspected the Elders of Zion were following him. Are you with me so far?"

The other men nodded, and Longarm continued.

"Dusty Wheeler had been confined to the Posada de San Francisco most of the time he was in Santa Fe. If he knew the Mex bad enough for them to start slapping leather on sight, Dusty must have known him from around the posada."

The county rider gasped, "Where Gertruda Moreno worked. So for all his blue blood and fancy vaquero outfit, he was likely working there as well and they *both* needed to get out of town before we got around to the usual questioning in more depth!"

Longarm said, "That's the way I read her. He'd have never run back to the Moreno spread after shooting it out with an Anglo, wounded or not. I know I ain't in command here, but if I was I'd have us split up some and cover more ground."

The undersheriff decided, "I'm fixing to saddle up and head on out to the Moreno place. You?"

Longarm said, "Railroad yards. Whether they'd meant to go on to El Paso or just give that impression, I'd best have some words with some railroad men."

They shook on it and, Cerrillos being a small town and Longarm being saddle-sore, he headed for the railroad yards on foot.

They had railroad yards and then some in the otherwise dinky desert town. From Trinidad, Colorado, down to Albuquerque to the south, the D&RGRR and AT&SFRR shared such railroad right of way as there was in a manner that looked like a double-track local line. Having fought at gunpoint for the bottleneck of the Royal Gorge up north, the rival railroads had learned it made for more fun and profit to get along. So there in Cerrillos as up the line far as Trinidad, the two railroads shared sidings, water towers, stock pens, loading ramps and such.

By now the sun was up and in his eyes, with the wagon traces and rail yards starting to blur some. Served by two rail lines, Cerrillos was more of a cow town than Santa

Fe to the north, and Longarm halted in his tracks to let some trail hands herd a score of woollies into an over-crowded sheep pen. Most New Mexican stock spreads raised beef for the nearby military posts and Indian agencies, whilst shipping wool, or sheep on the hoof, as a cash crop. The railroads charged by the pound, and pound for pound sheep sold for more once you got 'em there. The Western longhorn was duck-soup simple to raise but inclined to trim out as low-grade beef, better for corning or canning than as steak.

As one of the riders kicked the cage shut, Longarm stepped over to latch it. When the rider said, *"Gracias, amigo,"* Longarm replied, *"Por nada.* Do you expect an eastbound before the sun gets high enough to roast all that mutton in its own wool?"

The rider said, *"Sí,* less than an hour. Eastbound AT&SF way freight and local passenger combination up to Trinidad, where they'll be loaded aboard a highball to market. For why do you ask?"

Longarm said, "Just nosy, I reckon. You never know when you might want to ship some stock, or go for a train ride your ownself."

He strode on to the AT&SF freight and ticket shed for a smoke and a chat with the clerks on duty. Then he consulted his watch and ambled out of the yards and across the service road to the round-the-clock saloon serving a part of Cerrillos that never slept.

The place was nigh empty at that hour and there were no familiar faces there. Four gents who seemed to be together wore the mattress-ticking caps and overalls of railroad men. There were a couple of cowpokes, dressed like cowhands but paid to poke stock aboard the trains with their cattle prods. One of them looked Mex. An Anglo gent in a seersucker summer suit and straw planter's hat sat nursing a beer at a corner table. Nobody in a silver-trimmed charro outfit seemed to feel this was a good place to kill time.

Longarm ordered a tall draft and asked if they could build him a ham and cheese sandwich for breakfast. They could, and he ate it at the bar with a foot up on the brass rail, still stiff from over four hours in the saddle, mostly at a trot.

It took him another quarter hour or more to wash down the welcome snack, and then they all heard the whistle of an approaching train and everybody moseyed outside to watch the eastbound come in.

Longarm stayed on the plank walk in front of the saloon, in the shade of its board-and-baton awning, and lit a cheroot to wait and see as just across the way the train hissed to a stop, with its cattle cars naturally in line with the loading pens and the engine with its two passenger cars up the siding a piece. So when he saw the gent in the summer suit and big planter's hat mount the loading platform, Longarm strode faster across the way to follow him up the platform and called out, just as the galoot was fixing to board a coach car, "Hold on a minute, mister! I'd be the law, and I want to talk to you about that ticket to Lamy that you and you alone could have bought!"

The Anglo in seersucker dropped back to the platform with his legs wide apart as he went for his shoulder-holster Colt Lightning.

He was good. He was fast. He moved like spit on a hot stove.

But Longarm, starting out tense, moved even faster and, more important, aimed his gun better. So as something ticked the brim of his hat too close by half to Longarm's left ear, that planter's hat flew straight up in the air, as hats are inclined to do when their owners take spine shots.

As the white straw hat came down like a falling leaf, Longarm felt no call to fire again. Reloading as he mo-

91

seyed over, he muttered, "I'm sure sorry I killed you, Diamond Jack. For I surely wanted a word with you before they hung you!"

Holstering his six-gun, he got out his badge and pinned it on his denim bolero to save needless bullshit, and sure enough, when the conductor stuck his head out to stare down at them both, the first words out of his mouth was, "What did he do, Marshal?"

Longarm replied, "*Deputy* marshal, albeit federal. We're still working on exactly what he did, but he must not have wanted to talk to us about it!"

He was surrounded in no time by others bursting with questions. One of them being a posse rider who'd come down from Santa Fe with him, Longarm said, "Unless I've made an awful mistake, allow me to introduce you to Jack of Diamonds Walthers with an H."

The other lawman replied, "If you say so. But he don't look at all the way I was picturing him. What makes you so sure that's him?"

Longarm said, "Process of eliminating. Knew the late Dusty Wheeler shot it out with somebody he recognized as out of place in Cerrillos. Knew Wheeler hardly knew anybody anywhere in New Mexico and that he hadn't liked another tinhorn called Jack of Diamonds most of all. Knew that if I'd just gunned a man in a town this size I'd surely want to be out of it *poco tiempo*. Knew that if he missed that night train south with the law combing the streets for him he might figure on heading back up to Santa Fe by way of the short line north from Lamy. Didn't see why any honest Injun would need to buy a ticket to Lamy unless he had call to stay clear of the stage stop here in Cerrillos. So I asked at the ticket office and when they told me they'd sold exactly one ticket to Lamy all morning, I only had to figure out who bought it, with results you can see for yourself."

They both turned at the sound of pounding hooves, and

when the Cerrillos undersheriff and some county men reined in they naturally asked the same fool questions.

Dismounting to hunker over the remains, the undersheriff said, "You seem to have pinked him in the right thigh as well as dead center over the heart. Don't have no ID in this otherwise well-endowed wallet. I thought you said Jack of Diamonds was a flashy tinhorn with a mustache."

Longarm said, "That was then. This is now. Lately I keep running into all sorts of folk pretending to be something they ain't."

One of the county men he'd ridden down with said, "When we got out to the Moreno place we found nobody there at all. So we're still looking for that Mexican spitfire and her fancy vaquero in the silver-mounted charro outfit."

Longarm shook his head and said, "No we ain't. This is him. Only way to tell an Anglo from a pure white Spaniard is by the way they dress, talk and act. We heard tell Dusty Wheeler might have pinked the man he shot it out with, and this old boy was limping with a hole in his thigh. If you want more eliminating, why would an honest man with an innocent call for a ticket just up the line to Lamy draw on anyone who asked where he was headed?"

As others gathered 'round, Longarm said, "I could be wrong, of course. We'll know for certain once we show his head or better yet a photograph to others who met Jack of Diamonds Walthers with an H up in that posada lounge the night before that noisy poker game."

"And if it turns out you ain't wrong?" asked the undersheriff.

To which Longarm replied, "Oh, in that case we'll have solved the shoot-out at the Posada de San Francisco. With all them *others* still way in the middle of the air."

Chapter 11

Once Longarm had explained—more than once—what he'd eliminated, any lawman worth his salt could see what needed to be done. So they got cracking, and as word got out about what he'd done to their red herring the others made it easier by scattering far and wide, eliminating the sheep from the goats because anyone could see only the guilty had cause to run.

They ran far. They ran wide. And within days they'd been rounded up, because they'd run dumb and holed up with kith and kin known to a mostly outraged Mexican community.

Before half of them had been caught, those who hadn't killed anybody were singing like canary birds to save their own necks, and thus it came to pass that less than a week later Longarm was back in Denver, wishing there was an infernal ashtray on his side of Billy Vail's damned desk.

Oblivious to the way his senior deputy was treating his rug for carpet mites, Billy Vail said, "You done good. You et cucumbers and performed other wonders, and Governor Wallace thinks you have a crystal ball you ought to patent. So no bullshit, old son, how did you do it?"

Longarm modestly replied, "That process of eliminating you taught me. Once I figured why the same man would want to pass himself off as an Anglo tinhorn, a Mex vaquero and an Anglo businessman without that mustache, I saw the light."

He flicked more ash and continued, "We all of us see what we expect to see as long as what we're looking at acts like what we're expecting to see. Crazy Horse had wavy brown hair and blue eyes. But the trooper who bayoneted him up to Fort Robinson saw a wild Indian because he was *acting* like a wild Indian. The late and spiteful Dusty Wheeler saw me as a damned Jew because he didn't like Jews and didn't like me. Jewish folk or Irish Papists who get tired of Angry Saxons low-rating them find it easy enough to just change their names and pass for Angry Saxons. Jack of Diamonds Walthers with an H was really an Anglo-Mex they called Mike Robles around Santa Fe. They didn't know him in Cerrillos. Being blue-blooded Spanish and Scotch Irish in country where such folk have been mixing since the Santa Fe Trail was blazed back in 1821, he was as comfortable speaking English or Spanish and, like your pal, Marshal Harris, looked as Anglo or as Mex as he was dressed or acted."

Billy Vail waved his own stogie and said, "I got that part in your officious report. How come you knew before you had a positive ID that the killing at the Posada de San Francisco was a copycat crime?"

Longarm said, "Wouldn't eliminate no other way, once I determined an Anglo-Mex who'd come down from Santa Fe with Gertruda Moreno before I could talk to her was the Jack of Diamonds, working hard for us to be misdirected by a mysterious Anglo tinhorn. There was no way to connect him directly with the killing the next night, and before I caught up with him I'd caught the *posadero,* Pablo Montoya, in a big fib."

Vail started to ask a dumb question, recalled what

Longarm had put down on paper and nodded and said, "Right. It was dumb of him to try to sell you on that Mex gal vanishing during La Siesta when he knew damned well she'd lit out way earlier, with Robles, on the morning coach down to Cerrillos. But get to the apple core you had left after all that work with Ockham's Razor."

Longarm replied, "Like I told the excitable Gertruda Moreno, confession is good for the soul and as much as ten years off your sentence. But even before she and the others tied up some loose strings for us, the thrust of the plot was plain as puke in the collection plate as soon as I saw how hard they were working to convince us an Anglo tinhorn had to be mixed up in their inside job."

He took another drag on his smoke and continued, "The mastermind was the *posadero,* Pablo Montoya, the two-faced son of a bitch. Montoya had long been hiring that upstairs room to Bustout Sosa, another Anglo-Mex, for his high-stakes poker games. Old Bustout ran an honest invitation-only operation, and he was making out swell—sweller than Montoya thought fair. But when Montoya asked for more, old Bustout offered to take his beeswax elsewhere if he wasn't welcome at the Posada de San Francisco."

"So Montoya decided to take it all," Billy Vail said.

It hadn't been a question. But Longarm explained, "Montoya had read about the robbing of similar setups in other parts. But they all read as Anglo-on-Anglo crimes. So to make it look as if the same jaspers had done it in Santa Fe, he began by recruiting a nephew, Mike Robles. Like most of such extended Hispanic families, his kissing kin ranged from dark as any Indian to blue-eyed blond, and Robles was only asked to be a red herring. It was just old Dusty Wheeler's tough luck a knock-around Anglo-Mex he called a Jew boy knew how to take care of himself with a Colt Lightning."

Vail said, "Run that part about how they got the drop

on all those high rollers again. They must have known a thing or two about guns, right?"

Longarm said, "The gunplay came later, after everybody was dead. They had those other guests on the premises with ears, as well as planted memories of a colorful Anglo gambling man."

He flicked more ash and continued. "They killed them one by one when they arrived as usual one by one. Each victim was greeted by the flirtsome Gertruda and lured upstairs to that room at the end of the corridor. As each victim entered the dim-lit room he was jumped and burked by a trio of muscular stable hands."

"Burked?" asked Vail. "You mean like those Scotch grave robbers, Burke and Hare?"

Longarm pointed out, "Burke and Hare started as grave robbers, selling anatomic specimens to medical students. But they got tired of digging up bodies, and so they manufactured specimens by sitting on folk whilst Burke held their mouths and nostrils shut with his hands, resulting in no bruises on the delivered specimen. As Montoya's toughs burked each victim in turn, they were relieved of their table stakes and arranged artistic around the table. Once they had everybody and all the money to their liking, Montoya blazed away as he sauntered out the open door and down to the lobby, as guests and staff members came out to smell gunsmoke and report a heap of shit that had never happened."

Vail said, "It sounds crude, but it might have worked if you hadn't been such an eliminating cuss."

He took a drag on his evil-smelling smoke and growled, "So where does that leave us as regards the son of a bitch who killed that federal want and stole all them federal funds?"

Longarm made a wry face and said, "Back where we started on a colder trail. Governor Wallace says Santa Fe County gets to try those copycats for a purely local crime, and I'm trying to keep from picturing the real deal who killed that federal want in Tombstone as the flashy Jack of Diamonds. For all we know we're still after a balding dwarf or a circus fat lady."

Billy Vail sighed and replied, "If we're after *anybody*. Our own judges down the hall were far from thrilled when you were dragooned by name to serve in another jurisdiction. They bitched that we have enough on our own plate, and Judge Dickerson in particular got a sizzler off to Washington pointing out there's no proof that all these mass murders, similar as they sound, are the work of one gang."

Longarm shrugged and said, "Well, fair is fair, and His Honor may have a point. There's no proof Frank and Jesse pull every train robbery across the land, and Frank and Jesse copycatted the Reno brothers, who pulled off the first train robberies, the same ways, back in '66."

Vail said, "That's Judge Dickerson's point. You did a good job down Santa Fe way just now, but you did it for the sheriff of Santa Fe County, and he's got his own manpower. Unless there's some indication the next time's the work of that jasper who ran off with all those BIA funds, we may have to pass on it."

Longarm didn't answer.

Vail chewed his stogie like a growly yard dog and continued, "It happens that way, and you can't win 'em all, old son. We got so many man-hours to work with, and they don't expect us to catch 'em all at once. Frank and Jesse are wanted federal even as we speak, and Lord knows where that mean little shit Billy the Kid might be right now. We do what we can with what we have, and if we don't catch 'em, somebody else is bound to."

Longarm looked disgusted and asked, "Are you fixing to explain why boys and girls are built different next? I know the facts of life, boss. What do you want me to work on this afternoon?"

Vail ruffled through the papers on his cluttered desk before he said, "Summons to be served on a mean cuss out Arvada way. Chased the regular process server off his property with a ten-gauge Greener. Judge Dickerson says not to take chances with a dangerous fool who had his chance to come in and face the music like a responsible citizen. Judge suggests you just carry along a rifle that'll outrange his shotgun and if he still refuses to come quiet, end it with a bang."

So Longarm rode out to the hog farm in question, and faced with such a choice, the mean cuss allowed he'd only been joshing, accepted the summons and promised to be there with bells on.

So that left Longarm with the rest of the afternoon at his disposal just a few furlongs from the Arvada Orphan Asylum where Miss Morgana Floyd, a ravishing brunette, was the head matron and inclined to be weak-willed when it came to tall dark U.S. deputies if they were named Custis Long.

On this occasion, having read the recent newspaper accounts of events down New Mexico way, Morgana said she was sorry about the suspicions she'd been entertaining about him and a certain society widow, up on Denver's Capitol Hill.

When he said he hadn't been fooling with any Denver society widows down in Santa Fe, which was the pure truth when you studied on it, she replied she'd just said that and kissed him, French style.

So as he tended to his government remuda mount out in her carriage house, Morgana scouted up a junior matron to leave in charge of the little scamps whilst she hauled Longarm into her quarters to make it up to him, and by the time they'd come twice she was bawling fit to bust.

Thumbing a match head to light their mutual smoke as they snuggled bare-ass and sweaty atop the covers, Long-arm hesitated before he asked her how come she was so upset about coming twice. He knew that a man had to be careful about asking women why they were crying on any occasion.

Morgana said, "I was just considering how that horrid gossip might have come between us, Custis. When that spiteful Shirley Wertheim told me she'd seen you at that new comedy play, *Demon Rum*, with that snooty, fat, brown-haired bag from Capitol Hill, I made up my mind to never let you darken my door again!"

Longarm just lit the cheroot. He doubted she wanted to hear he hadn't found the sultry widow in question all that old or fat.

Morgana heaved a vast sigh and said, "Then I read in the *Rocky Mountain News* how you'd been down in New Mexico on a field mission all the time, and I'm too much of a lady, even naked, to repeat what I called Shirley the next time we met!"

Longarm replied, "Folk are always mixing others up. Your friend Shirley might have seen somebody who sort of looked like me or somebody saddled with the same name. Think how silly it would be to confuse the late Frank Leslie of *Leslie's Illustrated Newspaper* with Buckskin Frank Leslie, the terror of Cochise County, or a barkeep down yonder, leastways."

Morgana sniffed and said, "Shirley told me she saw you, yourself, with that society swell others saw you with at the opera that other time."

To change the subject, Longarm said, "You have my word I never took any gal to watch a comedy whilst I was in Santa Fe. And are you sure *Demon Rum* is a comedy, doll face? Seems I saw it advertised in the *Post* as a tragic melodrama."

She said, "Some say that's what makes it so funny. Folk got to see it trying to figure out if *Demon Rum* is meant ironic by a clever author or the worst play ever written by a fool who didn't know what he was up to.

Now that you're back in town, you can take me to it and the two of us can make up our own minds and talk about it afterwards, in bed."

He didn't see how he was going to get out of it. But, what the hell, if the fool play had been running that long the chances were all the ladies he had to worry about had already seen it or decided not to bother. So after he told her he'd see about picking up some orchestra tickets and snuffed out the cheroot, a good time was had by all.

When he rode back to Denver at quitting time, he dropped by the Larimer Street Theatre, where *Demon Run* had been playing, only to be told they were no longer running it. The gal at the ticket window, not a bad-looking redhead if you admired henna rinse, confided *Demon Rum* had been about the worst play they'd ever booked there. When he asked if it had been a tragedy or a comedy, she laughed and said, "Why not settle for *mystery*? I suspect the writer was out of his mind. More charitable folk figure he was drunk or eating opium. We had a short, profitable run as word got around and folk came to see for themselves. But the novelty wore off, and there's just no profit once half the seats are empty."

He thanked her and went on his way, not back to Arvada but up to enjoy the supper he'd been invited to on Sherman Street, running along the west rim of the rise called Capitol Hill, and that led to another story.

Next morning, back at the federal building on the floodplain of the South Platte with the rest of downtown Denver, Longarm climbed the marble stairs wondering why he felt sort of bushed and ambled on to the marshal's office, where old Henry and the young priss who played the typewriter out front said their boss had been in a spell and wanted Longarm to damn it report to him as soon as he got in. So he did.

As Longarm entered the smoke-filled, oak-paneled inner sanctum, chunky Billy Vail held out a sheet of stationery and growled, "Don't sit down. Read this letter, addressed to you by an admirer."

Longarm did. The typewritten message offered nothing a handwriting expert could use as it began . . .

DEAR SIR YOU KNOW-IT-ALL PEASANT:

HOW DARE YOU CONFUSE AN ARTIST WITH THOSE TREACHEROUS MEXICAN BANDITS DOWN IN SANTA FE? DID YOU REALLY THINK I WOULD STOOP TO METHODS HALF SO CRUDE? ALLOW ME TO OFFER YOU A HINT. I WORK ALONE. I DON'T NEED A GANG OF THUGS TO SUPPORT MY ACT. THAT BELLHOP IN TOMBSTONE WAS NOT WORKING WITH ME. HE GOT IN MY WAY AND I ONLY DID WHAT I HAD TO.

THE GREAT GARRICK

Longarm handed the brag back, observing, "So now we have a name for the real deal. I've heard that handle, the Great Garrick, somewhere. But it ain't anybody on our wanted lists."

"Until now," Billy Vail pointed out, adding, "I just showed that to the judges down the hall. As the firm but fair Judge Dickerson pointed out, poison-pen letters addressed to a federal peace officer are close enough to a federal offense for His Honor. So we're back in business, and they want you to bring the bastard in."

"He should have quit whilst he was ahead," said Longarm with a wolfish smile.

Chapter 12

The great Cloressa Chandler had gotten on some and hadn't been watching her weight, but a man did what a man had to do, and old Clo taught drama out to the university south of town.

She seemed pleasantly surprised to see him when he called on her at home with a box of chocolates. She said, "Custis, you shouldn't have!" as she tore off the ribbon to open the box and led him back to her setting room.

He'd known that when he'd bought the fool chocolates. She'd been something else in her day, but now her fine bone structure was buried in lard, her titian locks showed half an inch of dark at the roots and she'd put 'em up in an easier-to-tend-to bun.

After that, in deference to the early evening hour, she had on a dark kimono with nothing under it. You could tell when a hefty gal had nothing on under her kimono.

As she sat him down and popped a chocolate on her way to the sideboard for the wine and cheese she served to save brewing tea or coffee, the onetime star of the legitimate theatre asked in a kittenish voice what had brought him all the way out to South Denver. She said she feared he had more on his mind than her fair white body.

That was the pure truth, but Longarm gallantly replied, "I could have gone with my problem to this retired actor I know. But he ain't half as pretty as you, Miss Clo."

"You mean we're combining business with pleasure, as usual." She sighed, then returned to the sofa with a tray of wine and cheese to set it on a low-slung Chinee table and take up twice the room on the sofa as Longarm, despite his being no shrimp.

As she helped herself to more chocolate, Longarm confessed, "Well, as long as we're still upright, I did want to ask about an actor I think they call the Great Garrick?"

She smiled wistfully and said, "A little before my time, and I go back to Crabtree, Montez and Lind. In his time David Garrick was considered the greatest actor who'd ever lived. When he died in London Town during the American Revolution, more people turned out for his funeral than they had redcoats facing Washington. They never had a bigger funeral in Westminster Abbey until they buried Admiral Nelson there a quarter century later."

Longarm said, "We figured he had to be somebody important."

The no-longer-young actress heaved a vast sigh with her vast bosom and said, "I'm not supposed to, but I've often warned aspiring actresses long on looks and short on talent to get a man while they're hot and not waste the little time we have on kicking and scratching for that star on their dressing room door."

She popped another chocolate and continued, "Those stars fade so soon, and what do we have left? Who remembers David Garrick now? Heavens. Hardly a soul remembers *Edwin Booth*, and he's still alive!"

Longarm brightened and said, "I remember who Edwin Booth was. He was the elder brother of John Wilkes Booth, right? Wasn't he an actor too?"

She said, "My point exactly. In his day Edwin Booth starred as Hamlet over a hundred times. But now he's too old for such parts, and I fear his demented kid brother will be the only actor in the family the world will remember."

Longarm said, "We may be after another bad actor. Tell me why Garrick was so great."

She got to her feet again and with the surprising grace of many a fat gal crossed to a bookcase and brought a big picture book back to Longarm. She opened it to a centerfold of black-and-white sketches as she explained to him, "David Garrick died sixty years before portrait photography became practical, so we have to take it on faith that these were accurate makeup sketches."

Longarm took the book to stare down at a whole lot of different faces and ask which one was the Great Garrick.

The gal who taught acting said, "All of them. David Garrick was not only an accomplished actor in his own right but also the producer-manager of the famous Drury Lane Theatre. Whether to save on salaries or because he found it a worthwhile challenge, he often cast himself in more than one part in the same play, performing in various scenes as, say, the ghost of Hamlet's father, the evil uncle who murdered his father and married his mother, and the droll grave digger who hands Hamlet that skull to moon over. As you can see from those renderings of the same actor in different makeup, he could transform himself to seem old, young, handsome, ugly, kindly, cruel and so forth. He could pass for a country squire or a gypsy poacher. He often passed people he knew on the street and had a laugh at their expense when they failed to recognize him. He sounds like he was a lot of fun."

Longarm said, "I sure wish I could have seen him in action, on or off the stage. Which one of these faces might be closest to his own?"

She said, "Nobody can be certain. He was painted by Reynolds, Gainsborough and Hogarth, from life, and none of his portraits look like the same man. Even offstage he could change his whole appearance by what we of the theatre call *mugging*."

"You mean he made funny faces?" Longarm asked.

She sniffed and said, "Children can make funny faces; an *actor* can make himself or herself look completely different without appearing to distort his or her features. Given that innate ability, and adding a little in the way of costume and makeup, the Great Garrick could have gotten away with murder, if that had been his goal."

Longarm stared down at the bewildering choice of faces as he mused half to himself, "We seem to have us a modern student of such theatrical tricks who *has* been using them to get away with murder! It's too early to tell if the rascal just *calling* hisself the Great Garrick has half the original's talent, but if he does, I got a better handle on what we might be up against: a rubber-faced rascal who can make his fool self look like a bellhop, an invited guest to a private card game or even the *host* of the same if he replaced the man who sent out the invites or . . . Holy Toledo! What if an impostor just pretending to be a famous high roller invited other high rollers to a private card game, suggesting they bring serious table stakes!"

Longarm wasn't sure she was following his drift, and said, "Suppose I could turn into most anyone I wanted to look like and I blew into Denver as Bet-a-Million Gates, the wild-betting bobwire king. Suppose I announced a be-all to end all poker games at the Tremont House by invitation only and just sat there like a fat old spider to bite the heads off flies as they flew into my web."

She shuddered at the picture and asked, "What if the real Bet-a-Million Gates showed up to queer the do?"

He said, "Easy. I met up with him as somebody else before there was a word out about his hosting a game. In this particular case I'd pose as, say, a cattle baron in the market for a hundred miles or so of bobwire. Bet-a-Million don't really live by gambling. He sells bobwire by the mile as the most famous bobwire baron in the West, and all he has to do is break even with his wild-eyed gambling. But I digress. After I had Bet-a-Million dead in some cool place I'd turn into him and invite all the high rollers for miles to come into my parlor like the spider invited all them flies. Then, like those other killers down in Santa Fe, I'd lay everybody neatly out around the table, including Bet-a-Million Gates, and leave with all the money once I'd ventilated every corpse. I got to wire the coroner in Tombstone about Honest John Krebbs. It's been a spell, and none of the boys who sat in with him at the Cosmopolitan Hotel could still be all that fresh, but if there was some way to make sure Krebbs died the same night the others did . . ."

Then he grimaced, washed the nasty taste away with wine and shook his head to decide, "There ain't. I've talked to undertakers about their far-from-exact science. No two bodies decompose at the exact same rate. Provided you can keep a dead cuss cool, he's good for as long as seventy-two hours before he gets gamy enough to notice. After that, according to this expert I consulted on an outlaw who'd been dead a spell, stories of vampires, saints and such are the result of the unnatural ways nature can take its course with dead folk, depending on all sorts of odd chemistry. Dig up two dead soldiers buried side by side at Gettysburg after all this time and it don't seem fair, but one may look like he just fell asleep whilst the other one's turned to cesspool scrapings. You read in them detective novels how the docs can tell a murder victim died an hour and a half ago. But that just ain't so. Nobody's gotten to the victims of our self-styled Great Garrick to make an educated guess how long they were dead by the time the law showed up."

"How can they tell if someone who knows what he's doing gets there right away?" she asked.

Longarm explained, "They take the dead man's temperature, indelicate. Body cools about a degree and a half an hour. Coroner down to Santa Fe said none of the high rollers murdered by that Montoya bunch had been dead long enough to cause suspicion. Gent dead three hours or more can still be warm to the touch. Rigor don't set in earlier than four. It's more often six."

She said, "Brrr! It hardly seems fair, Custis. How do you lawmen ever catch killers if it's not as easy in real life as it seems in the mystery yarns by Mister Poe?"

He said, "Sometimes we don't. It ain't halfways fair. They get to pick the time and place, and most times things ain't halfway certain by the time we scout for sign. This jasper who delights in calling himself the Great Garrick could have been anybody on the premises at the time he did whatever he did. All the high rollers invited to his games, by whomsoever, have wound up in no shape to tell us what he done to 'em. On more than one but not every occasion he left dead hotel help in his wake. I figure the bellhops or waiters he killed must have busted in on something. When nobody did, nobody working there was killed."

Clo asked, "How about maids, chambermaids or waitresses?"

He started to josh about only a woman asking such a question, but then he said, "Lord love you, Clo, that might mean something! I got to check back and see whether the Great Garrick has a gallant streak or whether no gals were hurt because no gals were there to *get* hurt. I have to keep telling myself that job down to Santa Fe wasn't the work of the Great Garrick, so that flirty Mex gal don't count!"

He sighed and said, "I purely hate to scout for sign in dusty files, but somebody has to do it and Lord knows what he could be missing, all distracticated by those copy-cat killers down to Santa Fe!"

Her voice sounded suddenly older as she softly replied, "In that case you'll want to leave early tonight, right?"

Longarm wanted to think before he answered.

She said, "That's all right. I understand."

He'd known she'd understand. Like most natural men, he found variety to be the spice of fornication. But old Clo was spiced with a lot more lard than he'd found . . . spicy the last time they'd cuddled some.

But as he met her understanding eyes, he knew he had to do it. So he set his empty wineglass aside and took her in his arms.

There was more to take than there'd been the last time. Old Clo had put on a few pounds since he'd satisfied a heap of curiosity about fat women.

He got to shut his eyes when they kissed, and that helped some. For she kissed with skill as well as enthusiasm. So he bit the bullet and ran a hand inside her kimono, trying not to think about that joke about the midget and the circus fat lady lest he bust out laughing.

Then the nigh-as-fat Clo had her hand on his wrist and twisted her lips from his to murmur, "No, dear. Don't be angry. I know it was cruel of me to lead you on, but you kiss so sweetly and I sort of forgot myself."

Longarm tried not to let his feeling show as he kissed her again and said, "You're right. It *was* cruel. But don't it feel grand?"

She laughed and protested with her lips against his, "Let me go, you big silly, it's that time of the month and the curse of Venus is upon me, damn her to Hades!"

He'd already figured as much. He made a half-ass try, and when she sobbed, "I'm serious, damn it!" he reluctantly gave up, attempting to sound like a good sport, his finger bleeding, as he agreed it hardly seemed fair of Venus to come betwixt old pals like so.

She offered to help him out with a recital on his French horn, but Longarm allowed he couldn't enjoy himself that way with her left out. So they kissed some more and drank some more wine and he was out of there before ten, feeling as if he'd just rolled a seven.

For he'd learned a heap and it hadn't cost him as much as he'd been prepared to pay, if he had to. And seeing he didn't have to, he caught himself whistling as he moseyed over to Broadway to catch a horse-drawn streetcar back to the center of town.

Of course, being a natural man and hence heir to the contrary ways of mortal flesh, he had a raging hard-on by the time he was halfway there, and 10 P.M. on a workday night was a hell of a time to tell a man you had the infernal rag on, even if you were sort of chubby!

He contemplated getting off short of the Capitol grounds and trying his luck up on Sherman Street. But it was after ten and life was just too short to argue with women, even when they had light brown hair and twenty-four-inch waists without a corset.

So he got on the far side of Tremont Place and legged it down to the Parthenon Saloon to see if that new barmaid still laughed at his jokes.

She wasn't there to laugh at shit. It was her night off. So Longarm was left to laugh at himself, and did so till he wound up choking on his needled beer.

"What's so funny?" asked a familiar voice in the startled crowd.

Longarm turned to see Reporter Crawford of the *Denver Post* staring at him the way a kid stares at a firecracker that's failed to go off after you've lit it on the Fourth.

Longarm got hold of himself to say, "Just considering human nature and how contrary half our plans pan out."

The stocky newspaper man in the checkerboard summer suit had naturally been reading out-of-town papers.

So he asked if they might be speaking of that mass murderer who was still at large.

Longarm laughed again and said, "Let's eat this apple a bite at a time, old son. Right now I'm still wondering how this evening is fixing to turn out for *me*. It ain't too late to try my luck at the Black Cat; it ain't too late to go back to the office and paw through some dusty damned files. And I know that no matter which way I go from here I'm likely to wish I had done the other, along about three in the morning."

Chapter 13

Nobody ever got to the office earlier than Marshal William Vail of the Denver District Court. So he was thundergasted when he showed up an hour before anyone else was supposed to to find his senior deputy's tweedy length stretched out on the leather chesterfield in his reception room.

As Longarm opened a sleep-gummed eye to regard him morosely, Billy Vail asked, "What happened? Has your long-suffering landlady evicted you at last for sneaking gals up her back stairs?"

Longarm swung his boots to the rug and rubbed at his face as he asked in a conversational tone, "Did you know that Le Mat outfit over in Paris, France, uses that fool metric system?"

Vail snorted, "Of course they'd use the metric system, making guns in Paris, France. What's all that got to do with the price of eggs in China?"

Longarm said, "I've figured out the murder weapons of the Great Garrick. Hasty coroners opined they'd dug out distorted .40-caliber slugs and the birdshot from a 16-gauge fowling piece. But one old pro who knew what he was supposed to be doing measured exact and came up with roughly .41-caliber balls cast in a two-piece mold. The roughly number 20 birdshot could have been fired by any gauge, but I make it .66 caliber as we measure bores. A Frog gunsmith measures everything in milly meters and they never come out just right. I add it up to a brace of Le Mat horse pistols, one in each hand. You know the pissoliver I'm talking about?"

Vail snorted in disgust and said, "Hell, no, I was too young for the war. Jeb Stuart was the only one of the Confederate Cavalry officers who rode with a French Le Mat—swamping cap-and-ball pissoliver with, you're right, nine revolving chambers firing them queer Frog bullets from a top barrel and a muzzle-loading shotgun forming the axis of the cylinder to discharge from the center of the same. Such antiques have long been out of fashion with gun slicks loading with modern brass cartridges, but I follow your drift! Did a murderous son of a bitch front-load and cap a pair of such weapons in advance, he'd commence the festivities with eighteen pistol rounds and two shotgun blasts at his disposal, close range!"

"He ain't never taken on more than eight or ten men at a time," Longarm pointed out, adding, "Aside from deadly, a pair of Le Mats would be easy enough to conceal, one under either coattail. No fowling pieces to worry about no more."

Vail said, "I like it. The numbers and curious shit dug out of dead men adds up to a brace of Le Mats for me. What else did you dig out of Henry's files, old son?"

"You ain't going to like this part at all," Longarm said with a sigh, fishing out a smoke as he continued. "Our self-styled Great Garrick seems to be the master of disguise he brags on. Aside from the unusual ammo, there's nary another common bond, save for maybe one. He's hit east and west, north and south. Sometimes he's gotten in and out without any of the hotel help offering any assistance as to how he got in and out or what he looked like.

On a few occasions members of the hotel staff have wound up dead or missing. *Missing* don't mean *dead* when a transient hotel is by definition a hotel where folk come and go."

"You say you did find one common bond, though?" Vail asked.

Longarm said, "I might have, at the cost of considerable back-checking and paper cuts. On the other hand, it could be what the census takers call a statistical artifact."

"A statistical what?" asked Vail.

Longarm explained, "Figures you can add up to false conclusions as you take a census. More white folk have indoor plumbing than colored folk or Indians; Chinee eat more rice than the rest of us; ergo, shitting indoors bleaches the skin and eating rice turns it yellow. But I have established that the Great Garrick has yet to harm a woman, and we do know there are lots of whores and chambermaids to be found in the sorts of hotels all his crimes took place in. There's more than one high-stakes gambler of the she-male persuasion, such as Poker Alice or the late Madame Moustache. So should we credit the cold-blooded killer with a gallant streak or just figure the gals have been lucky?"

Vail decided, "Let's leave that an open question. Must be hundreds of such games held every night across considerable territory."

Longarm lit his cheroot, blew smoke out his nostrils like a sincerely pissed-off bull and said, "That, too. The son of a bitch as ever has the damned initiative. I have searched in vain for some way we might guess ahead and stake a likely target out, but I just ain't found it. The Great Garrick gets to strike when and where he decides to; we get to try to cut sign as we clean up after him. There has to be a better way!"

"If there was I'd have heard about it," Billy Vail said sighing, then added, "The average outlaw is too dumb or

114

lazy to hold a steady job. Half the time he fails to break in or cracks a safe with no money in it. He gets falling down drunk and fights with his pals over women or just to be fighting because he's a mean son of a bitch. And it takes us forever to catch him because he hits at random where we ain't expecting and runs with a hell of a head start."

Longarm replied, "I just said that. Even as we speak high rollers all across the land are sending out invites to unfriendly little games we'll never hear tell of unless they turn out fatal for somebody. Ain't no way we could stake 'em all out even if we knew in advance the games were being held. One of the things that gave Montoya's copycat crime away was that he robbed those Santa Fe high rollers less than a month after the Great Garrick hit in Tombstone. I figure, at the rate he's been striking for real, we ought to be in the clear till roundup time. But he's sure to hit most anytime after, most anywhere in the country, and don't that cheer you up just awful?"

Vail shrugged and said, "We know Frank and Jesse figure to rob a bank or a train somewhere in this great land of opportunity. We know Billy or Dave are fixing to steal a cow somewhere along the Pecos most anytime now. I just said the cocksuckers have the initiative. If we can't cut sign the next time the Great Garrick strikes, we'll cut sign sooner or later. That's the way the game's been played since Robin Hood was poaching deer in Sherwood Forest."

So that was how they played the game against the Great Garrick, and seeing they were open for other business, Longarm's next field mission was up to Fort Collins, where another federal want had been spotted in a house of ill repute.

His name was Eli Milland. They called him The Eel. He was more famous as an escape artist than he was for interfering with the U.S. mails. The last time he'd done that they'd sentenced him to ten at hard, and after a mere eighteen months of making little rocks out of big ones, he'd busted out, robbed another post office and vanished for a spell.

But like his fish-brained namesake, The Eel was not a heavy thinker, and so since nobody had arrested him lately, he'd surfaced in Fort Collins as if nobody was looking for him serious.

Picking him up would have been a chore for a junior deputy, save for three other traits Eli Milland was known for: He seemed to have eyes in the back of his head, he could move faster than a fly swatter and he had sworn they'd never take him alive again.

Fort Collins was about sixty miles north of Denver by crow. Longarm got there a tad slower by rail, arriving late in the afternoon. Not aiming to look like a moon calf who'd visit a cathouse in broad daylight or even early in the evening, Longarm checked into a nearby transient hotel, where he tried to appear more cow than he'd been for a time by dressing for the part in faded jeans and a new black sateen shirt to go with his borrowed Boss Stetson and asking the bellhop if they had action to offer on the premises.

The teenaged bellhop regarded him with that superior expression the city slicker reserves for the rube as he said, "This ain't that kind of hotel. If you spy any bleach blondes or bottled redheads on the premises, be advised they're actress gals, not hookers. We got the cast of the play about demon rum staying here."

Longarm replied, "Do tell? Well, it surely is a small world. I've been aiming to see that play one of these days. But getting back to friskier action . . ."

The bellhop pocketed the quarter Longarm had handed him as he shook his head and said, "Red Light Row is the other side of the tracks, and if our town law sees you wearing that six-gun on the streets of Fort Collins it'll cost you a five-dollar fine."

Longarm said he'd leave it in his hired room with his bedroll and added, "Got handed the shovel at the Middle Fork west of Boulder and ran my final pay up better than double in a friendly little game aboard the Burlington Line. So I mean to unwind some before I sign on for the fall roundup at your famous Lazy B. Your Red Light Row would be where a famous parlor house called Madame Zenobia's might be found, right?"

The local boy laughed and said, "It would. But Madame Zenobia's is too rich for *your* blood, cowboy. They ask two bits a drink at the bar and the French gal who offers Arabian Nights asks ten dollars a trick."

Longarm whistled and responded, "Thunderation! What could any fancy gal do that was worth ten dollars?"

The kid shrugged and said, "Hard to say. I'm too romantic-natured to pay. But I understand they'll do you three ways for two dollars at Madame Du Prix, so take my advice and steer clear of Madame Zenobia's!"

Longarm allowed he'd think about it, and he did, once he'd gotten rid of the kid. He unsnapped his double derringer from his watch chain and put it in a hip pocket of his jeans before he hung his six-gun on the bedpost for the time being.

His plan of operation called for him to establish himself as another knock-around drifter, known around town, before moving in on The Eel. It didn't take as long as one might think when you were out to fool an often convicted stickup man instead of British Intelligence.

He figured that long before he got close enough to The Eel to matter The Eel would have noticed him. Fugitives like Milland spread silver about to make sharp-eyed friends in low places. Once he'd established himself as a harmless, not too bright drifter, Longarm meant to have someone drag him to Madame Zenobia's for the plucking.

There was no way any stranger could ask to be admitted without The Eel hearing about it before they let him in.

Milland was boarding on the top floor with hot and cold running whores at exorbitant rates. He was forted up good, and they wanted him taken alive. So there went simply smoking him out. The tip had come from another federal want who'd sung for a lighter sentence after being taken alive. So there went Longarm's chances for a personal introduction. Knowing where his man was and aiming to take him alive, he had to get in and get the drop on The Eel, all by himself.

It didn't figure to be easy. It never did. But he had the one edge that was always with the offensive. He had the initiative.

As everybody who'd ever set down to write a tome on tactic had figured out, the side on the defensive had everything *else* going for them. It took ten times the strength and numbers to establish a good position than it took to hold it. So time after time, as at the Alamo, Constantinople or, say, that McSween stronghold in Lincoln Plaza, digging in and forting up had seemed the smart way to go.

Constantinople was the classic example of what was wrong with the notion. Nobody had ever held a candle to that Byzantine Empire when it came to digging in and forting up. Their whole military strategy had been based on the best defense they could manage, with mighty walls and weapons that rained hellfire and brimstone down on the forever attacking Turks.

So time after time the Turks had attacked and time after time they'd gotten beaten back, and had they had a lick of sense they'd have ceased attacking.

But they had the initiative. It was up to them and them alone what time of the day or season they attacked. So they attacked and lost, attacked and lost, until in 1453 they won, just once, and there was no Byzantine Empire anymore. Results at the Alamo and the McSween house had been much the same.

Of course, Longarm didn't want to get shot up as had those Turks, those Mexicans or even some Murphy-Dolan riders. So whilst the time he moved in on The Eel was his to choose, he was still working on his approach.

He was fixing to mosey on down to the taproom and establish himself better as a harmless local sport when he heard what sounded like a poetry reading coming at him through the wallpaper. He moved over and put an ear to the same. Some gal in the next room over was rehearsing what sounded like the reading of a poem or a play in verse, such as Mister Shakespeare had written. She was trying to make herself sound young and innocent as she let fly with . . .

"Father, pray, father, if you won't come home,
Then give us what's left of your pay.
The house is stone cold and the lamps have gone
   out,
And we haven't eaten all day!"

"Aw, shit, ain't that sad?" muttered Longarm, chuckling, as he turned from the wall and continued on down to the taproom. When he got there he found others bellied to the bar ahead of him, some wearing stage makeup and raggedy costumes cut with shears to look that way. As he ordered a needled beer, the older actor nursing a plain draft with his face made up red of nose smiled friendly and suggested, "I take it you haven't seen our presentation of *Demon Rum,* young sir, or if you've seen it the message failed to get through to you."

Longarm smiled and allowed he'd heard of their famous play but hadn't gotten around to it yet.

The friendly cuss made up as a drunk reached in his

119

raggedy coat to say, "Allow me to present you with two free tickets, then. Bring the guest of your choice. God knows we need at least a *couple* of people in the audience tonight!"

Chapter 14

Longarm started to say he had other beeswax that evening, but you never knew, so he took the tickets and put them away with a nod of thanks as he observed, "I know I got no right to ask. But don't you theatrical folk usually put on your costumes and makeup at the theatre?"

The actor already made up as a drunkard nodded but said, "Publicity. The theatre's just a block away, and the effect of strolling over in costume is something like one hopes to arrive at with a circus parade. May I ask how you seem to know so much about the theatre? Have you ever studied acting? On second glance, you rather resemble a man dressed up for the role of a range rider. The hat's a nice touch."

Longarm laughed and said, "I'm just an old cowhand, but I did 'tend a drama class in school one time."

The actor stared thoughtfully and asked, "Why did you drop out? You have the looks, the stature and the voice of a juvenile lead. Surely they don't pay you more for herding cows!"

Longarm found it easier to laugh this time before he said herding cows ran in his family and introduced himself as Bones Baxter, late of the Middle Fork down Boulder way.

The older man said he answered to Archer Bannerman, producer, director and star of *Demon Rum.* He added, "We've a slot for a tall, dark and handsome pillar of strength, if you'd like to read for the part. The one we had quit in Denver, and I fear his replacement is a tad short and squeaky. The pay is a share of the profits, and I cheerfully confess that can vary a lot. I naturally pay travel and living expenses, out of my own pocket if need be. So what do you have to lose? How much do they pay you for herding cows?"

Longarm sipped some suds as if considering this outlandish notion before he replied, "Forty and found for a top hand, which I consider my ownself. With the fall roundup coming in, some outfits may be willing to pay more, temporary."

Bannerman said, "Nonsense. In a bad month with us your cut will top forty dollars. I'll admit we bombed in Denver, but we did better than *that.*"

He sipped at his schooner thoughtfully and added, "People in Denver think they're too sophisticated for the message of our temperance play. Do you know some came to laugh and jeer? Up this way, where our audience goes to church more regularly—"

A shorter man about the same age, wearing no makeup, came over to cut in with, "It's going on that time, Mister Bannerman."

The impresario nodded and introduced the shorter cuss as the stage manager, a Froggy Hummel. He did look sort of like a frog—a real frog, not a Frenchman—when you looked closer.

Bannerman said, "I've just been trying to interest Baxter here in the part of Reliable Steve, Froggy. What do you think?"

The stage manager stared at Longarm with his big pop

eyes and said, "Anyone's an improvement on poor Will Penny! Will's miserable in the part, both ways. Baxter here has the looks, and he may have the range. So why not give him a shot at Reliable Steve and let Will get back to what he does best, shifting scenery."

Before Longarm could explain he'd come up this way to hire on at the Lazy B, some other cast members came in. One was a gal around thirty in a blond Little Eva wig and Alice in Wonderland pinafore. Bannerman called her over and said, "Esperanza, my dear, I'd like you to meet our new Reliable Steve, Mister Baxter. We're going to have to do something about his cowboy nickname." Then he turned to Longarm to add, "Miss Esperanza O'Hara is the ingenue Reliable Steve saves in the last act. We'll expect you to help Will Penny change some scenery early on, when you're not on. It's a small albeit important role, and we all have to pitch in."

Esperanza asked where Longarm had appeared before. He truthfully told her he'd never appeared anywhere on stage all that much. He doubted they'd count that time he'd shot it out with a crook in that opera house as appearing on stage.

She tried not to sound unkind as she told Bannerman, "Nice shoulders, good baritone voice. Have to hear him read for the part before I can say he has any projection."

Bannerman said, "You heard the lady, Bones. Let's get on over to the theatre. Can't let you go on tonight with no rehearsal. For all his faults, Will Penny knows the part, and the lines are set in verse. No ad-libbing."

The grown actress gussied up like a teenager said, "You ought to learn your lines within twenty-four hours. If you can't you're not a trouper. I can help you with them, when there's more time. Right now we have a show to put on. Let's go."

So they went, with folk along the way staring at them as if they were riding elephants with rings on their fingers and bells on their toes. Fort Collins was that sort of a town. The sun was going down behind the Front Range as they marched into an alley and entered the Strand Theatre by way of its stage door. Longarm had been backstage a few times in his travels, so he didn't stare like a fish out of water, and that made the others feel as if he might not be.

The three-sheets out front set their opening night half an hour after sundown. So some few denizens of Fort Collins were already buying tickets out front. But nobody was seated in the audience when one of the junior cast members peeped out from behind the stage curtain. An older actor said not to do that. Longarm already knew you weren't allowed to ever whistle backstage either.

Bannerman sent somebody to fetch a script for Reliable Steve and told Longarm, "Want you to read your lines as if memorizing poetry for a school recital, over and over till the lines just flow. That's how come we thespians of the old school prefer plays written in verse. You'd do better seated in one of the boxes tonight, watching the stage business that goes with your lines."

Longarm started to say he had to get it on down the road. Then Esperanza O'Hara had him by one elbow and seemed to want to lead him off somewhere. So he went, as most men would have. She smelled of lilac water and woman as well as greasepaint.

She hauled him after her through a confusion of sandbags on ropes and around drops of canvas painted to look like all sorts of scenery to where he got turned around some. Then they were on a stairway up to a second-story hallway and she led him out into one of those theatre boxes like the one Lincoln got shot in, and, sure enough, he had a swell view of the stage below. Save that the curtain was down and nothing was happening.

As she sat him down in a plush chair, Longarm said, "Miss Esperanza, I keep trying to say this and nobody listens. I want to see your play. I may even want to be *in* your play, but I have this . . . appointment in other parts this evening."

She said, "The play will be over and we'll be back at the hotel by ten. Can't your other business wait that long?"

Longarm started to say no. But as soon as you studied on it, a house of ill repute was just getting started around ten and a real Bones Baxter would have no sensible call to balk at such a golden opportunity for a life upon the wicked stage in place of herding for Chrissake cows. So he went with the current and said he'd stay, and they must have wanted him to because the next thing he knew she'd given him a big, wet kiss.

Then she was gone before he could cop a feel. So he leaned back in the plush seat to study the part of Reliable Steve as folk commenced to slowly drift in down below. Nobody had ever asked Longarm for those two tickets back. He wondered idly why he felt glad about that.

There was just enough lamplight to make out the neatly block-lettered lines they wanted him to memorize. He knew he wasn't supposed to laugh; he knew poor old Bannerman didn't think he was producing a comedy. He had to wonder where Bannerman's sense of humor or proportion was.

After he'd tried in vain to read the lines of Reliable Steve without grinning like a shit-eating dog, he folded the script and put it away for the time being. There were no signs posted. But nobody down below had lit up. So he just sat there, dying for a smoke but trying to do right as he stared down like an eagle bird and now and again saw somebody staring back up at him. The box seats cost more. Nobody else seemed to have sprung for one. He wondered if word had gotten around Fort Collins about *Demon Rum.*

There were as many empty seats as filled ones when

the curtain finally went up and everybody clapped and whistled. The scene on stage was set in a saloon Longarm would have avoided unless he'd had a damned good reason, and there was old Bannerman, leaning against the center of the bar whilst the barkeep—who was also the villain, Longarm knew from reading ahead—got him to drink some more.

Nobody laughed until Esperanza O'Hara appeared in the doorway in that pinafore to recite in that little-girl voice the poetic lines entreating her father to come on home or at least let her have some of the money he'd been drinking away. Some of the audience tittered; Esperanza pretended not to notice.

She repeated her pleas until Bannerman swung around to glare at her and shake his fist at her, reciting back . . .

"Go 'way, begone, oh forward daughter!
I need no advice from such as you!
My thirst desires more than water!
Without my rum the world seems awfully blue!"

Most everybody in the audience laughed. Some clapped or whistled. And so it went from there, downhill, with Longarm feeling embarrassed for the folk on stage, albeit they never let on they noticed laughter in the wrong places as the temperance play, or a parody of one, dragged on in tortured rhyme. The familiar plot wasn't all that funny. Everybody knew unfortunate families like the one in *Demon Rum* and everybody knew how they usually turned out if the breadwinner of the family didn't get a hold on his drinking before he lost his damned job and they wound up in a *real* fix.

But the spectacle of actors on stage saying all their lines in verse—bad verse—was just too comical for folk to pay mind to the plot. Longarm knew that Shakespeare and other early playrights had written in verse so's often

126

illiterate cast members could keep track of their lines. But you had to listen tight to notice that Hamlet or Romeo were saying things that rhymed, and good actors of the modern stage tried to deliver such lines as natural-sounding conversation. Whoever had written *Demon Rum* hadn't been as clever as Will Shakespeare, and his play just sounded silly.

Longarm idly wondered how many of the actors knew this as they went on getting laughed at and even booed. Esperanza O'Hara looked too smart by half not to know. The jasper playing the barkeep-landlord-villain who meant to make Miss Esperanza, as Fair Violet, marry up with him recited his lines with an expression that reminded Longarm of a class clown kept after school. Most of the performers were likely has-been or never-were actors who needed the work and went along with whatever the hell poor Bannerman thought he was doing.

It was possible, of course, that Archer Bannerman knew exactly what he was doing. A not too original, lackluster temperance play that people came to hoot and laugh at likely sold more tickets in a season than if they'd been taken serious. Lots of old-time actors put on airs and pontificated about their so-called art as if they meant it. An actor was by definition a grown man or woman who went on playing "Let's Pretend" after most children had outgrown the game.

Fair Violet gave up trying to recite sense to her drunken father and went home to console her siblings and poor old mother in a house with no coal in the stove, no oil in the lamps and no food on the table. Some of the audience decided to go home as well.

Others cheered as the villain-barkeep-landlord confided to Fair Violet's father that he'd always had a yen for the gal and so he was willing to stake her drunken dad to all the rum he could drink for as long as he lasted in exchange for his daughter's hand in marriage.

Then the curtain came down for a spell so's they could change scenery, and more of the audience went home without waiting to see what happened next.

What happened next, as the curtain rose to reveal the interior of a cold and hungry hovel, was that things got worse, in verse.

The drunken father had managed to give his daughter's hand in marriage for enough demon rum to kill him.

With everybody weeping and wailing over him, the villain showed up to claim his prize, and Longarm moaned, "Aw, shit, I can't!" when his character of Reliable Steve barged in, sort of squeaky-voiced, to declaim in verse . . .

"Unhand that maiden fair and true!
You lowly knave with vile design!
For she shall never marry you!
If she will have me, she shall be mine!"

"Marry the taller one, girlie!" cried a voice from the rear, and everybody laughed. But the cast soldiered on, as Longarm said to himself, "Not one time if I have any reason, for Gawd's sake!"

Since he and everyone else could see that the play was winding down, they all stayed put for the ending, with Reliable Steve, holding hands with Fair Violet, assured her . . .

"That wretched figure on the floor,
Is not the dad you used to know!
Your father's gone, he is no more,
T'was demon rum that laid him low!"

So everybody clapped like hell and the curtain came down whilst Longarm just sat there, marveling to himself,

"Old Morgana down in Denver was correct—that has to be about the worse play ever written!"

He rose to join the stampede out the front lest somebody catch him and make him read for the part of Reliable Steve. Outside the night was still young, and he figured he'd timed it about right. Around ten was a natural time for a cowhand who'd had a run of luck to drift into a famous house of ill repute, belly up to the bar and sort of play things by ear whilst he figured out how to get upstairs to The Eel. Or to get The Eel to come downstairs to him. So he headed for Red Light Row on the far side of the tracks, lighting up at last as he chuckled and said to himself, "Reliable Steve my ass and elbow. That'll be the day when I go on the wicked stage to recite bad poetry with everybody laughing at me. . . ."

And then as he shook the match out, he stared thoughtfully at the winking ruby porch lamps in the distance to mutter, "Hold the thought, old son. We may have just struck color. There's more than one way to skin a cat, or perhaps to wriggle an eel out of its hidey-hole!"

Chapter 15

Madame Zenobia, as she called herself, was a hard-eyed handsome woman of a certain age and uncertain ancestry. Some said she was a woman of color passing as white. Some said she was Shanty Irish passing as Gypsy. Others held she was some sort of Oriental, like the original Queen Zenobia in Syrian times. She didn't care what others thought, as long as they paid for her services.

She provided most any service folk were willing to pay for, from honest liquor at her bar to pleasures defined as crimes against nature by the statute laws of Colorado. If a man on the run wanted to hole up and play with himself, Madame Zenobia had just the place for him to do so, at her price. She charged what she considered fair prices for good services and gave good services because she considered herself a professional. Madame Zenobia had neither liked nor disliked anyone for quite some time.

Her place was a good place to get laid because her girls gave a man what he asked for with no argument. Her place was a good place to hide out because she and her girls were careful about who they let in downstairs.

The tall, dark stranger in the Boss Stetson and sateen shirt had come in around ten-thirty and hadn't shown much interest in anything but the action at the bar. Madame Zenobia had already sent a bouncer across the tracks to nose around over yonder. The stranger seemed to be nursing needled beer. So he wasn't a drunk, and he'd been jawing with Lucy behind the bar but hadn't expressed any desire for closer companionship. So what was he all about?

She sauntered over to him, a disquieting vision in see-through black lace, to ask him point blank if he knew he was in a whorehouse.

Longarm ticked the brim of his oversized hat to her as he confided, "I ducked in here to avoid a woman who wants to teach me poetry, ma'am."

Madame Zenobia smiled thinly and replied, "I've heard of some perverse desires in my time, but reading poetry to a man sounds just disgusting. How much have you had to drink since you started out this evening, cowboy?"

He truthfully replied, "I ain't drunk. I just escaped from a poetical play about getting drunk and this other lady wants me to hire on as her juvenile lead, Reliable Steve. I keep telling them I ain't no actor but the real actor they had playing Reliable Steve up and quit on them down in Denver and . . . Never mind, you had to have been there."

Madame Zenobia asked, "Are we talking about that new play in town, the one called *Demon Rum*? I heard it's a comedy."

He said, "It is, unintentional. Folk were laughing fit to bust tonight, and I for one ain't about to go on stage and have strangers laugh at me."

She cautiously said, "Neither am I, but seriously, cowboy, drinks at this bar are priced break-even to encourage our regular trade; I don't make any profit down here. So if you don't want to go upstairs with the girl of your choice to do anything to her you choose—"

"Say no more," Longarm cut in, reaching in his jeans as he continued, "I just ain't up to slap and tickle this

131

evening after a day it would be indelicate to talk about. So let me treat Miss Lucy right and I'll be on my . . . Hold on, I forgot I had these on me."

He produced the box-seat tickets and handed them over as he explained, "Picked these up earlier at my hotel, meaning to take in the play everybody warned me not to miss. But next thing I knew them actors were out to recruit me as Reliable Steve and I got to see the fool play free. So now I got these two swell box-seat tickets, and now they're all yours."

Madame Zenobia stared down at the tickets he'd crossed her palm with as she murmured, "What am I supposed to do with these, for heaven's sake?"

He said, "Sell 'em. Give 'em to a couple of your gals or good customers if you don't want to go to the show with a pal and have a good laugh. I'd offer to take you, but I've already been and I'm ducking the Fair Violet."

The worldly whore blinked and asked, "The fair what?"

Longarm struck a pose and recited . . .

"Fair Violet, if you're ready now,
This humble shack is not for thee!
You'll eat three times a day, I vow,
If you will fly away with me!"

Madame Zenobia laughed like a teenager and said, "Go for it, cowboy! You've a natural talent for comedy! You say they really spout such lines in that play about demon rum?"

He nodded and said, "Some lines are funnier, unintentional. But I see I've been wasting your time with my foolishness, so I reckon I'll be on my way and let you make an honest dollar."

Some of the other gals and more than one John were drifting over now. Madame Zenobia invited Longarm to stick around and spout more poetry, but he laughed off the invite and quit whilst he was ahead, with everybody there smiling at him. As he ducked outside, a rat-faced shorter cuss came in, not looking at him. As the door shut behind Longarm, Madame Zenobia asked, "Well, Rooster?"

Rooster said, "Staying at the Majestic across from the rail stop with that theatrical troupe. Barkeep says he seems to be in with 'em. But the bellhop has him down as a cowhand looking for work herding cows."

Madame Zenobia shrugged her bare shoulders and said, "Wonders never cease. Every other year or so somebody in pants tells this girl the truth for a change."

If Longarm couldn't hear her, he could just about guess what was going through her mind about now as he ankled on across the tracks to the more seemly parts of Fort Collins.

There'd been no way to cast the bait closer to the fish he was after. Plopping unexpected bait too close could spook a wary mossback or an eel on the prod. The odds were better than fifty-fifty Madame Zenobia would give the tickets to somebody else, or sell them. But when you cast no bait you caught no fish, so what the hell, and there was always the chance a bored and cooped-up owlhoot might be inspired by laughing whores to break cover far as the Strand Theatre just across the way.

It was worth a try, and a whole lot safer than pussy-footing up those whorehouse stairs for a sure as shooting shoot-out.

He got back to his hotel a tad after eleven, avoided the taproom and went directly upstairs.

It didn't work. Esperanza O'Hara was tapping on his door by the time he'd hung up his borrowed hat. He let her in; he figured he had to. When she said she wanted to go over his lines with him, he told her he didn't want to be Reliable Steve.

133

She wasn't wearing her blond Little Eva wig; her natural hair was blue-black. She wasn't wearing her Alice in Wonderland pinafore; her natural figure filled out her Turkish toweling kimono more womansome. She pushed her way in to demand, "Give me one good reason, Bones! It was one thing for a professional actor to drop out after we bombed in Denver. But you are a forty-dollar-a-month *cowboy*, for heaven's sake! Don't you have any ambition to improve your station?"

Bones Baxter Longarm asked, "What's wrong with a top hand's station? Herding cows is my occupation. Spouting poetry on stage will make me feel a total fool!"

She dimpled and said, "Oh, my Lord, you have stage fright! That's it, isn't it? You're reluctant to go out on stage and face the audience!"

He replied, "I ain't reluctant. I ain't going to do it. Reliable Steve is supposed to be in love with Fair Violet, poetic, and to tell the truth that poetry sounds right silly!"

She sighed and said, "You're right. We've asked and asked Archer to let us declaim in prose. He won't hear of it. He insists all the classic plays since Euripides have been written in verse."

A dumb thing Longarm had read popped into his head, and without taking time to think he joshed, "Euripides and I'll rippa doze."

She laughed and said, "I was right—you're more than an illiterate cowhand. You took drama in school and dropped out because you suffered stage fright. It happens to lots of drama students. Froggy Hummel wanted to be a character actor, not having the looks for leads, and he's quite good in the part of Richard the Third—in rehearsal. He simply balks at going on in front of an audience."

Longarm said, "I'm with him. I could never spout mush at Fair Violet in front of a hundred strangers sitting out front! I'd feel a perfect fool."

She insisted, "How do you know? We haven't rehearsed a single line. Do you have something to *hide*, Bones?"

He did, but he naturally asked, "What would I have to hide, ma'am, aside from not wanting to act the perfect fool?"

She said, "It's just occurred to me you might be . . . wanted somewhere. We had a spear carrier for a while who'd escaped from a chain gang back East and never saw fit to put that on his application."

Longarm said, truthfully enough, "I ain't wanted by the law. I just don't want to act the perfect fool."

She moved closer to say, "Work with me, Bones. What will it hurt for us to play that last romantic scene with nobody watching at all?"

She put her hands on his sateen shirt to husk, in verse . . .

"I've never had so grim a day!
And suddenly I feel so queer!
Away, away, take me away!
And kiss me, kiss me, Steve, my dear!"

He laughed like hell and kissed her. She tried to bust loose, then decided to kiss him back. French. So neither said anything as the two of them wound up across the bed with her fumbling at his belt buckle whilst he determined she was wearing nothing under her kimono.

They both knew better than to let their lips come unstuck before he was in her with his sateen shirt open and his jeans down around his boot tops. She wrapped her bare legs around him and hugged him deeper into her being while she tore his shirt trying to take it off him.

When she felt him ejaculating inside her, she purred with her lips against his, "Me too. Don't you want to get undressed, dear?"

He did, and so did she, and once they were naked as

jays atop the rumpled bedding, it seemed only natural to go at it some more. So they did, and when at last he stopped to catch his second wind, Esperanza said it was his turn to tell her how fond he was of Fair Violet, in verse.

He said he'd study his lines some more, but explained that he needed a breather and that a smoke might not hurt. So they wound up pillow-talking with one cheroot to share betwixt them, and since she seemed to think his playing Reliable Steve was settled, it seemed a mighty dumb time to dispute her.

He wasn't ready to tell her who he really was.

He knew that neither she nor any of her troupe were in cahoots with Eli Milland. But two could keep a secret when one of them was dead, and the three most rapid means of communication were telegraph, telephone and tell a woman. So he knew that his best bet would be to stall for time or even go on stage till he saw whether The Eel was going to take the bait or not.

Reliable Steve wouldn't be called on to recite his lines until the last act, and from backstage you had a clear view of the box seats those tickets were good for.

As they snuggled and smoked, she confided that Esperanza wasn't the name she'd started out with and agreed *Demon Rum* was an awful play. But not unlike that other actress, the blond Modesty Bevers, the black-haired Esperanza seemed to prefer acting in a bad play to waiting tables in the grandest restaurant in the land.

He blew a smoke ring towards their mingled bare toes and said he'd long wondered about why so many actors seemed to hail from Hebrew, Gypsy, Irish or Welsh families, next to the Angry Saxons who made up most of their audiences.

She said, "That's easy. Outsiders grow up to be either toughs with chips on their shoulders or natural actors.

136

When your background's not Anglo-Saxon Protestant in this country, you can clan up with your own kind and dare anyone to call you names in your own neighborhood, or you can learn to pass."

He asked where acting skills came into just behaving natural.

She said, "Acting natural when you're the new kid in school isn't natural—it's acting. You teach yourself what acting coaches call stage business. You happily share meat on a Friday with the friendly Protestant girl who offers to split her lunch with you. If you're a Jewish kid, you may bite into a ham and cheese sandwich as if it was the most natural thing in the world. You laugh at jokes you don't get if all the other kids are laughing at them. If you're invited to supper and they say grace as you've never heard it said before, you watch what the others at the table are doing, and if you act the same way, nobody ever asks when your people left the auld sod. They accept you as *belonging* because you act as if you belong, and after a while you learn to use other stage business to belong in an English drawing room comedy or a melodrama about demon rum because you seem to have a natural acting talent."

She made a wry face and said, "It takes a lot of work. Being the new kid in school just gives you a head start."

He said, "I reckon I must be a natural actor too. I've noticed nobody stares at you curious when you wear one of them beanie hats at a Hebrew wedding or make the sign of the cross at a Papist funeral."

She took the cheroot from his lips and reached down betwixt Longarm and herself to get a better hold on the situation as she made a lewd suggestion.

So the next thing they knew they were going at it dog style, and as she arched her trim spine to take it deeper, the born actress lowered her head to the pillows to recite

"Oh, Steve, my dear,
I feel so queer.
With father lying dead!
What shall we do?
It's up to you!
Where I shall lay my head!"

Longarm laughed like hell and, getting a grip on either hipbone as he spread his bare feet on the rug for purchase, recited back . . .

"Fair Violet, if you're ready now
This humble shack is not for thee!
You'll eat three times a day, I vow,
If you will fly away with me!"

And so with nobody else laughing at them but themselves, they had the short role of Reliable Steve committed to memory by the time they'd come a few more times, and besides, what the hell, the play was so bad and the lines were so awful that nobody was likely to notice if he got some wrong, right?

Chapter 16

The next day, with their clothes on, they went over their lines in the hotel dining room for Archer Bannerman. When he asked Esperanza if she'd taught "Bones Baxter" about rhubarb, she smiled like Mona Lisa and said there hadn't been time because they'd been concentrating so hard on their lines.

Bannerman explained to Longarm, "When you forget a line, say 'rhubarb.' "

"How come?" asked Longarm, adding, "No offense, it makes no sense."

The old trouper replied, "Exactly. The audience will hear it as 'rhubarb,' and since that can't be what you said they'll assume you said something that made sense and they missed it. When actors on stage want to stage a crowd scene they simply say 'rhubarb, rhubarb,' with perhaps one of them saying 'celery, celery, celery,' see?"

Longarm laughed. Bannerman said it wasn't funny and to pay attention if he wanted to become an actor. Bannerman said "actor" as "act toar" and seemed to feel it had being a cowboy or a railroad engineer beat.

Later, Longarm felt the fool in Reliable Steve's top hat and tailcoat when they paraded over to the theatre. But at least he got to pack his six-gun, tucked in his belt, under the silly costume.

Once they were inside the Strand Theatre with nobody gawking at them, the ever-inquisitive lawman learned more than he likely needed to know about putting on bad plays.

The folk out front and most of the stagehands worked their regular. The old-timer who guarded the stage door in from the alley had been doing so since the Strand was built, he bragged. The Bannerman Company had a few key backstage hands who bossed the theatre crew and pitched in to help with heavier work. Froggy Hummel managed everything Bannerman didn't and seemed to have a clearer notion what things were about. An even shorter and uglier cuss called Whispers MacUlric got under the stage to stick his head out a trapdoor near the middle of the footlights, where the audience had no idea he was. The footlights were candles set in sort of mirrored cups to shine up at the actors on stage. Whispers was there in case any of them forgot a cue or line. The poor soul had memorized the whole fool play and could whisper in one direction loud enough for the actors to hear without letting the audience in on the dodge.

It was Whispers who told "Bones Baxter," suspecting his stage fright, to picture everybody in the audience sitting on a chamber pot, taking a shit.

When Longarm laughed and asked how come, the gnomish Whispers told him, "How ridiculous could *you* look, up on stage, next to people shitting in public?"

Longarm said he'd try to remember that and as long as they were on the subject, and seeing Whispers seemed to know his beeswax, Longarm asked him how he felt about all the lines in the play being recited as awful poetry. He asked, "Wouldn't the lines sound more sensible in common prose?" Whispers nodded soberly and asked, "Who'd pay to listen to them? *Demon Rum* is a piece of shit. Father Dear Father has a drinking problem, and we know where we're going from there in the first act. Everybody out there shitting in public has watched more than one drunk in the family slowly sink in the west. They come to *laugh* at a situation they've forever found depressing. Archer Bannerman knows what he's doing. We're not showing one hell of a profit, but we're slowly but surely getting ahead, and one of these days, with the money to work with, the Bannerman Company will stage the bee's knees of a show!"

He looked away and mused, "Money isn't everything. For one thing, it can't buy poverty."

Longarm agreed and scouted up Will Penny to learn about the ropes he had to pull backstage when he wasn't on it being Reliable Steve.

Knowing which ropes to pull, and when, was more important than being strong enough to pull them. Those sandbags dangling all about were the counterweights that made it possible for one man to raise or lower big "flats" of canvas painted to look like city streets, forests, insides of houses, saloons and such. Will Penny had amusing tales to tell of curtains going up to show pioneers facing Indians in fancy French ballrooms or poor Miss Cinderella sweeping up after her cruel stepsisters out in the woods.

The time they had till curtain call went swiftly, because it was new and interesting to Longarm. Then folk were filing in to sit and shit in those seats out front. Longarm knew he wasn't supposed to peek out at them through the curtain, or to whistle. So he worked around to the wings and found he could see the box seats those tickets went with, catty-corner and across.

He cussed when he saw they'd just been occupied by Lucy, the whore who tended bar at Madame Zenobia's, and the rat-faced bouncer, Rooster.

It could have been worse. There could have been nobody up there in those expensive seats. So Longarm muttered, "The show must go on, and if I was hiding out in a whorehouse I might want somebody to scout ahead before I broke cover."

So he decided to be a good sport and stick out the run of the show in Fort Collins. If his bait failed to draw The Eel out by then, he'd have to just go in and get him. Asshole-puckering notions like that could do wonders for stage fright.

He didn't have to go on stage until the last act, of course, and he was anxious to get it over with. So it didn't bother him all that much and he never fluffed but one line. That was when Lucy, up in the box, recognized him under the light makeup of Reliable Steve, waved at him and told the whole audience, at the top of her lungs, she'd served him drinks and he could hold his liquor better than Father Dear Father.

Since a good many men in the audience knew where Lucy served drinks, a voice from the rear yelled, "It's all right, boys, if he drinks at Madame Zenobia's. He only *looks* like a queer!"

Somebody else yelled to shut up and let them get to the damned end. So they did, and everybody clapped and whistled when the curtain came down with Fair Violet in his arms at last. Longarm could only hope nobody was able to see she was kissing Reliable Steve in the French fashion.

Then everyone was clapping "Bones Baxter" on the back and telling him he was a born actor. Archer Bannerman said they'd have to come up with a better stage name than *Bones,* for land's sake.

Later that night, Esperanza confided with a tongue in his ear that she'd never laid anyone named Bradford before. To which he could only reply he hadn't either, so a good time was had by all as the newly christened "Bradford Baxter" and Esperanza O'Hara recited their lines in

142

some positions they hadn't gotten around to before. He enjoyed a hearty breakfast after all that drama coaching with a couple of winks thrown in.

But at curtain call when he sneaked a peek at the eel trap he'd set, he saw Madame Zenobia and a whole bunch of her whores filling all the seats up in that box. On the other hand, he knew she'd paid for them. So Lucy and and Rooster had given the awful play good reviews indeed.

The madame and all her working girls clapped and whistled when Reliable Steve came on stage to save Fair Violet from a fate they customarily asked a dollar for. But when the curtain came down Archer Bannerman said he'd done a swell job. So what Whispers had said about Bannerman knowing what he was doing was likely true.

That night in bed with Esperanza, Longarm sensed they were both starting to show off and he knew they'd soon be getting to the stage where it started to feel like work. She'd ask where this thing they had going was likely to lead a gal who had to think of her future.

But as any kid who'd ever fished for eels could tell you, once you had your baited hook in the water you had to just hang in there and let time and tide run their courses. The Bannerman Company was booked into the Strand Theatre for a two-week run, and a man could stand two weeks in bed with the same gal when she was young, and pretty, too.

As long as he could keep her talking dirty instead of *much*. So far, Lord love her, she'd been content to crack him up by reciting the lines of Fair Violet in ways they'd never been written. You had to give credit to a gal who managed to switch "Ah, whist, 'tis time to part!" to "Aw, shit, did you just fart?"

But he had to wonder how long they'd be getting along so fine when, next afternoon as they got dressed for the show, she suddenly asked how come he was stuffing all that hardware under the tailcoat of Reliable Steve.

He said, "Force of habit, I reckon. Man gets used to riding open range with a side arm and—"

"Bones, I'm talking about those handcuffs," she cut in, adding, "How often did you handcuff cows in your range-riding days?"

He said, "Oh, those? Forgot I had 'em. They go with the gun. I served as a part-time deputy sheriff down to Boulder County. What do you care if I sort of balance the weight, Fair Violet? You ain't wanted by the law offstage, are you?"

She demurely replied she'd murdered her last two lovers, and they went down to grab an early supper before the show.

She never said another word about the six-gun and handcuffs she'd seen. That meant she was thinking about them, Longarm knew; when women didn't ramble on about things they'd seen, you knew they were thinking about them. Longarm had to do some thinking too. He had to decide whether she'd be less likely to spill his beans if he leveled with her and swore her to silence or if he should hope for the best without giving her anything to spill.

He didn't recall what he'd had for supper by the time they were parading over to the theatre. He kept telling himself he was at that stage where the kid with the dough-ball on the bent pin gives up and moves down the bank to try another stretch of creek just as the wily old fish was fixing to strike. Fish got old and wily by not striking at every fool kid's dough-ball. He had to give his fish, in this case an eel, time to eye his bait from all sides and decide he had nothing to lose and mayhaps even some laughs to gain to break the tedium of a worried life on the Owlhoot Trail—unless, of course, he'd already lit out for another hidey-hole.

144

That was something for a kid with his bait in the water to study on. An outlaw on the run was by definition not a man who planted sweet corn out back and watched it grow. It was even possible The Eel had left his Fort Collins hidey-hole before that other outlaw told the law about it. Longarm had to consider he might have been going through all this bullshit for nothing.

Then they were filing in out front, and this time, when Longarm risked a peek, there was nobody up there in that fucking box at all!

Whispers MacUlric sidled up to him to ask, "What's going on? Who are you so worried about out in the audience? Does Esperanza know about her?"

Longarm said, "It ain't like that. I invited this gent I know to come see me act on the stage."

As he caught the knowing look in the promoter's eye, he added, "It ain't like *that,* neither. You were right the first time. You don't miss much, do you, Whispers?"

The gnomish older man smiled thinly and replied, "I'm paid to watch you great actors like a hawk and make sure you don't trip over your own feet or somebody else's lines. You're on edge—I can tell. What's so all-fired important about your invited . . . Jesus H. Christ, have you been dickering with an *agent* after *one* performance?"

Longarm laughed and assured his fellow member of the company he wasn't out to go into business for himself, just yet. Whispers muttered darkly and said he had to duck under the stage, adding, "Don't go off on your own before we've had time to get to know one another, cowboy. You do have the looks, the voice, the stage presence and mayhaps the raw talent. But you need some trouping under your belt before it'll be time to talk about a serious role for you in a real play."

Longarm said, "Sure"; it was easier than arguing. They parted friendly and Longarm was about to go back and

145

help Will Penny when he had himself one last look at the catty-corner box seats.

Two of them were occupied now. A man and a woman, both dressed to the nines for a night on the town, were up yonder waiting for the curtain to rise. The woman was likely a high-priced whore. The man was Eli Milland.

The Eel had changed his duds since the last time he'd held anybody up. But he hadn't had the sense to shave his Vandyke whiskers. If Longarm had been on the run with eyebrows like that, he'd have at least trimmed them some.

Crawfishing back from the wings on that side, Longarm moved across the back wall of the theatre, drawing his .44-40 along the way. As he made it to the far side, Froggy Hummel overtook him to demand, "Have you gone crazy, cowboy? Put that fucking gun away and go help Will Penny move that bar on stage."

Longarm said, "I can't. I ain't a cowboy. I'm the law. Federal. On my way to make an arrest. The want I'm after is up in box eight, alone with his lady of the evening. You'll get to read all about it in the papers, win or lose, and it's been nice talking to you, Froggy."

But the short homely stage manager tagged along at Longarm's side as he replied, "Knew you were more than a cowboy. Let's go. I'll back your play, and they'll read all about *that* in the papers!"

Longarm asked, "Are you packing a gun, Froggy?"

The stage manager said, "Of course not. But I know how to handle myself in a rhubarb."

As he made his way to the foot of the stairs, Longarm said, "So does the gent up in box eight. They say he favors a brace of Schofield .45s, one under each arm in its own shoulder holster. If you really want to back my play, stay here and make sure nobody comes blundering into the gunsmoke if things commence to get confusing. I'm out to take him alive; he has sworn he'll never be taken alive. So you can see how things may tend to get confusing, right?"

Froggy gulped and decided, "I can. So perhaps it will be best if I stay here and make certain you gentlemen are not disturbed as you settle the matter between you."

Chapter 17

Longarm had been born good-hearted and raised by kind parents. Kind country folk who'd raised everything they ate instead of bringing it home from the market.

When you raised everything you ate you scooped out a pumpkin or gutted a chicken with little thought about the feelings of either. You dug a peck of potatoes or you slaughtered a hog as need be. Your fruit trees had to be pruned. You marked and branded a calf and cut off its balls. Horses were broken to saddle or sold for glue. In sum, you did what you had to. And so growing up country gave a lawman certain advantages when it came to doing what had to be done.

Eli Milland had come down from under the mansard roof of Madame Zenobia's facilities with his nerves all atingle and his guns loaded six in each wheel. As he sat in box eight, both guns were out in his lap, with his hands on their grips. But as *Demon Rum* got going with others snorting in total disbelief at the pathetic poetry, The Eel began to chuckle, dryly at first and then more carefree as, like many a cooped-up cuss before him, he started to marvel at how good it felt not to feel so cooped up. The whore at his side had been there the night before with Madame

Zenobia and others. That gawky cuss who'd started all this by offering free tickets had turned out to be an actor after all; he was fixing to come on later and save the Fair Violet from a fate worse than death.

So Eli Milland caught himself laughing along with everybody else as the tragic tale ran on, apparently in dead earnest.

Longarm waited until Father Dear Father fell down on stage and got a good laugh before he made his move. He reached as high as he could and got a grip on the curtains behind them. Then he parted the curtains to bring the heels of both fists down.

Hard.

When you hit man or beast in the head hard enough to stun 'em instead of just pissing 'em, you could hurt them serious. But a good blow to the base of the neck on either side could knock 'em cold without putting 'em in the hospital or the grave. So he hit The Eel from the right and his lady of the evening from the left and had the two of them stretched out on the corridor carpeting behind the curtains before anybody in the audience noticed.

By the time either was coming around, he had The Eel's wrists cuffed behind him and a booted foot in the center of the rascal's spine, with his .44-40 covering them both.

As what Longarm had done sank in, the dazed Milland called him a sneaky son of a rabid mongrel bitch and a misbegotten cocksucker. The whore contented herself with asking what the fuck had happened as she sat up, holding on to the side of her neck.

Longarm told her, "I just knocked you out for a spell, ma'am. You're in the aisle behind the box seats, and it's going to be all right. I'm the law—federal, and I don't have anything federal on you. So just you rest easy till you get yourself together and I'll see about getting one of the stagehands to carry you back across the tracks."

As she stared glassy-eyed in the dim light of the narrow corridor, she complained, "I already had a gentleman to escort me, and why do you seem to be standing on him, good sir?"

The Eel hissed, "Because he knows I'll kill him the second I get back on my feet, the yellow-bellied cur!"

Longarm said, "Compliments will get you nowhere, Mister Milland. I'd be proud to fight you fair but I had orders to take you alive, and we both know there's no way to take you fair *alive*."

"That's for damned sure, you cocksucking motherfucker!" snapped the man he had at his mercy.

So Longarm put a little more weight on his spine as he answered, not unkindly, "Watch your mouth—ladies present. I'm fixing to haul you to your feet now, and then we're heading backstage along this second-floor level."

As he did so, he motioned with the muzzle of his six-gun to tell the whore, "You first, ma'am. You go through that curtained archway at the far end and down the stairs, where you'll meet up with a Mister Hummel and ask him to stand clear as I herd Mister Milland down. Then we'll see about getting you safely home and Mister Milland safely to jail for the night."

So that was the way they worked it, with not one but four stagehands seeing the lady of the evening home and Eli Milland stored in the Fort Collins lockup whilst Longarm bade a fond farewell to life upon the wicked stage at the cast party held in honor of Bradford Baxter.

Everybody seemed to take his deception in good grace, save for Will Penny, who wasn't looking forward to playing Reliable Steve again, and Esperanza O'Hara, who smiled like Mona Lisa with a toothache and allowed she wanted a word alone with him, later.

More than one member of the company said they'd known all along he'd had some acting experience. Longarm was too polite to point out that crooks and lawmen

150

working undercover had to have better-than-average acting skills because they were risking more than boos and catcalls when the fluffed a line.

Rex Cunningham, who played the villain but just looked like a fat man without his makeup, asked how come Longarm hadn't arrested Madame Zenobia for aiding and abetting a federal fugitive.

Longarm patiently explained, "I could have, and there was an outside chance we'd prove in a federal court that Eli Milland had told her he was a federal fugitive. There's no federal statutes covering her other wicked ways."

"But surely you could put her out of business," insisted the man who was supposed to know how to be a villain.

Froggy Hummel laughed, raised his glass in a mock toast and explained, "This is only his second season on the road. He still thinks the world is run on the level."

Longarm nodded wearily and replied, "As stage, road and property manager, you get to deal with such local graft as there may be, right?"

Froggy said, "Always, at every opening. With luck we get off with giving away a wad of free tickets. When they ask for too big a slice of the gate, we don't open in their fair city. They usually know how far they can push it. But they always push."

Longarm explained to the villain of *Demon Rum,* "If the town law here in Fort Collins thought I was fixing to cut off such a source of income, he'd tell me to guard my own fool prisoners for all he cared. Us federal lawmen work with local lawmen on a live-and-let-live basis. They give us a hand with serious outlaws and we don't don't mess up any good things they may have going for themselves, see?"

Cunningham sniffed like a priss and demanded, "How can we taxpayers be expected to respect professional law officers who wink or turn their backs on situations like this town's notorious Red Light Row?"

Longarm shrugged and said, "It's the professional law-man rather than an outright crooked politician who knows how much slack he can cut what the French call the *dem-imonde* with a sardonic smile, because they been dealing with 'em longer."

He sipped some suds and continued. "There's always going to be businesswomen such as Madame Zenobia, whether you ask 'em nice to do business in one part of town and mayhaps contribute to the political party of your choice or try in vain to run them out and only run them out of sight and your control. You're going to have gam-bling—reasonably honest where you can keep an eye on things, or out of sight where you can't and bad things happen. The churchgoing farmers currently running Kan-sas just voted the state dry. You can still belly up to the bar in the Long Branch or that Alhambra in Dodge be-cause the lawmen would have way more policing on their hands if trail herders took to buying moonshine in back alleyways after dark."

Cunningham sniffed again and demurred, "Next thing you'll be telling us that no such noble local lawmen would dream of taking graft from the keepers of brothels, card houses or saloons where they're against the law."

Longarm snorted, "Ain't you been listening? Of course they take graft, if only in the form of free theatre tickets. Graft is the grease that keeps civilization running smooth—in moderation. You don't want too much graft any more than you want too much grease gumming up a locomotive. Maybe I should have described the notion as *equity*. That's lawyer talk for 'let's not get carried away with the letter of the law.' Some laws are impossible to enforce the way they were written."

Rex Cunningham said he didn't understand.

Froggy Hummel laughed and said, "Let it go, Long-arm. You'd do better trying to sell Darwin's notions of evolution to to a Sunday school teacher—and what's the prize if you convince *this* lovely creature?"

Most everyone there but Rex Cunningham laughed. He said, "Aw, you all know I'm right."

The hell of it was, Longarm knew, the fat priss *was* right, as right and wrong were measured by children in an ideal world run on the level, as Froggy had suggested.

As one of those founding fathers had pointed out when they got down to the nuts and bolts of the Constitution—it had been Adams or Madison, as Longarm recalled reading—in a Garden of Eden inhabited by saints, no governments would be needed. But since all men were created equal with all sorts of odd or sneaky notions, you had to have rules and regulations overseen by folk who weren't saints their ownselves. So they'd designed a system of checks and balances that ran with, say, the rough reliability of a water mill when compared against the picky Swiss watch efficiency of Mister Bismarck's new Prussian Empire—and for that matter, if Mister Bismarck's notions of government were so efficient, how come so many High Dutch folk kept coming to America?

Longarm felt no call to lecture on civics or to give away trade secrets of the working lawman. So he didn't go into how tough it would be if they cut no slack with and never got any tips from the whores and gamblers who found it smart to support their local sheriff. Longarm knew that the case of the Great Garrick would have been solved by now if the murderous bastard had been hitting the usual back rooms and card houses. The killer was working outside the range of the usual talk around the fires along Owlhoot Trail. The wise-ass high rollers who'd elected to hold sneaky games by invitation only might have all still been alive had they just cut the town law a slice of the profits. Killers were brought to justice pronto in places as corrupt as, say, Bodie, Dodge or Tombstone when the lawmen on the take knew what in blue blazes was going on.

Later that night, as promised, Esperanza had a word with him, dog style, about his leaving her to go on getting saved from Rex Cunningham by Will Penny when she didn't fancy either of them in that position.

He turned her on her back and hooked an elbow under either of her knees to show her how sorry he was. She allowed she took some comfort in knowing she'd seduced a famous lawman instead of a merely handsome cowboy, but she couldn't help wishing he'd have stuck around for the flush times that were coming, when they'd be playing Omaha during the fall sales. Archer Bannerman, as a showman who'd been playing the West a while, had promised them all the moon if they'd stick with him through roundup time.

Sharing a smoke with Longarm in the rosy afterglow of some fine rutting, Esperanza idly asked, seeing he'd know, how come all the cattle outfits rounded up all their cows at the same time. To her way of thinking, they'd have made more money in the end selling off a head or two of beef at a time.

He put the cheroot to her lips as he explained, "They would, if no other costs were involved. But to sell one cow or a thousand, you have to produce the same where the buyer can take it off your hands. Cows are not kept under the counter in a drawer. You make money raising cows by turning a four-dollar calf loose on open range to graze and grow a year or more and wind up with enough beef on the hoof to sell for forty dollars west of Chicago to buyers who can ask sixty or more back East. It adds up profitsome, but you can see nobody makes near a hundred dollars on the sale of one cow. After that you have to pay a cowhand at least a dollar a day and found. So when you send him way out on the open range to round up a cow, he may as well round up all he can."

Esperanza took the smoke from her kissy lips to ask if that surely did not result in a glut on the market.

He said, "Sure it does. So does picking all the apples or reaping all the wheat. They call such doings the *harvest*. Can't be helped. When the human race invented agriculture way back when, they traded picking a berry hither and a mushroom yon for eating regular off the stored harvests of a year or more. If it was possible, how would it look if a farmer ran out to his south forty to reap a bushel of wheat on one baker's demand?"

She laughed at the picture but asked, "How do you store a cow if it's better to round them up all at once, and why does everybody round them up at the same time?"

He said, "Coming in off the range, a grass-fed yearling might trim out stringy and tough. The buyers resell them to feedlot operators who feed 'em grain as they laze around doing nothing but getting fatter. After that, once they're slaughtered, the meat will keep a spell in cold storage, corned or canned. A steak you et this week might have roamed the range a year or more ago. It's a business, not a bunch of kids in big hats and furry chaps playing tag with cows for fun. Bannerman's right about fall being the flush times out our way. Makes more sense to sell a cow for what you can get after a summer of free-ranging, because it costs to get a cow through the bitter winters on the high plains, if you manage to."

Next morning when he traipsed over to reclaim his federal prisoner, Longarm found The Eel still threatening to kill him and all his kin out to kissing cousins, first chance he got.

As the Fort Collins turnkey opened up, Longarm said, "Turn around and let me cuff you."

The Eel sneered, "What if I don't want to?"

Longarm sighed wearily and said, "Don't matter what you want or what I want. I got to take you down to Denver, now. You can come along like a man or I can borrow a straitjacket from the lunatic asylum, strap you to a litter and let the reporters see you getting off the train like a pathetic crybaby. So what's it going to be?"

The Eel turned around and let himself be cuffed.

As they were leaving, Longarm said, "I'm pleased to see we're fixing to get along. We'll be riding in a private Pullman compartment. Long as you behave sensible I'll be proud to share my smokes and spring for a sandwich and soda pop."

The Eel grudgingly allowed he'd heard Longarm was firm but fair, so what the hell.

Longarm figured he'd wait until they were aboard and more relaxed before he asked if a man who'd been spending time on the darker stretches of the Owlhoot Trail had heard about any invitation-only games along the same.

Chapter 18

A lawman was firm but fair because he knew his onions. Lawmen who were in the game to carve notches in their pistol grips or show prisoners who was boss weren't professional peace officers—they were bullies packing badges. So Longarm treated Eli Milland neither better nor worse than the situation called for, and by the time they were halfway down to Denver the ornery cuss was sipping soda through a straw and commenting on the passing scenery sort of wistfully, as a man who wasn't going to see much of the great outdoors for a spell.

They'd both worked with cows in their times, and agreed the coming roundup would lead to good times in the cow towns after a wetter summer than usual, making beef prices unusually high. One of the reasons smart lawmen were firm but fair was that a lawman could never learn too much, and it paid to ask the professional opinions of unreconstructed outlaws.

The Eel allowed he'd heard about those unfriendly endings to friendly little games of poker by invitation only. He opined the killer calling himself the Great Garrick was a bad actor indeed and nobody any of the hard-cased professionals he'd ever ridden with would take on.

He explained, "Don't take me for softhearted. I still aim to kill you and all your kin if I ever get the chance. But how can you trust a two-faced killer? How do you know a man who'd look another man in the eye and lie to his face to get the drop on him wouldn't do you the same when time came to split the swag? It's one small step from cold-blooding a stranger who never done you wrong to double-crossing a rider you just throwed in with for fun and profit, see?"

Longarm said, "I follow your drift. But how do you figure the killer who styles himself after a famous actor is two-facing players who trusted him?"

The Eel said, "Only way it works. I've been following his career in the papers. You don't bust in on gun-toting gamblers and catch a whole table of 'em off guard. You got to be *sitting* at the table, trusted as another player, when you make your play. You wait till there's a break in their attention, like somebody's just won the pot and they're watching him rake it in, before you produce a brace of antique cap and balls with eighteen rounds of outlandish bullets and a couple of barrels of birdshot and just start blazing away."

Longarm frowned thoughtfully and said, "There was nothing in any *papers* about outlandish bullets, pard."

The Eel said, "He's packing Le Mats with them metric French bullets and queer-gauge shotgun chambers that come out around .66 caliber, as white men measure. One of the papers said they dug .41-caliber slugs out of a high roller in Wichita last February. Witnesses have counted more than the dozen shots a two-gun man gets off with a brace of six-guns. What do you want, egg in your beer?"

Longarm thanked The Eel for his professional opinion and bought sandwiches. They barely had time to eat them before they were in Denver, the trip down from Fort Collins not being all that long. Guards from the Federal House of Detention were there to meet the train, so they parted polite if not exactly friendly, with The Eel still promising to kill Longarm if he ever got the chance.

By the time Longarm reported in at the federal building, the sandwiches he'd had aboard the train were wearing off. But duty called, and Billy Vail had less patience than his innards, he figured.

He saw he'd guessed right when Vail's first words to him were "It's about time you got here! Did you enjoy your paid vacation up yonder in Fort Collins?"

Longarm sat down uninvited, having already lit up, and calmly replied, "I was under the impression you wanted Eli Milland brought back alive. He's sound as a dollar and threatening my life over to detention, even as you're chewing my ass. Didn't you get the telegraphed report I sent last night?"

Vail grudgingly said, "I want a regular report in full, in triplicate, by the end of the week. I swear, you get sillier every time I send you out in the field. A grown man, for Gawd's sake, putting on greasepaint to go on stage in a dumb-ass morality play?"

Longarm flicked ash on the rug and said, "I could have just set fire to Madame Zenobia's and shot him as he came out the door, like you ordered me to. My acting career up yonder wasn't all that long, and it gave me ideas. How come the bad actor calling his fool self the Great Garrick gets to have all the lines and enter or exit stage left or right whenever he decides to? What if we were to write the script for him? What if we had a famous high roller set up an invitation-only private game with bodaciously higher than ever table stakes and then—"

"Why don't we commence to patrol the Owlhoot Trail from high in the sky in flying machines?" Vail cut in, adding, "Teach your granny how to suck eggs or come up with grand notions this old dog has never considered?"

He waved his evil-smelling expensive cigar like he was trying to shake out the smoulder and elaborated, "Such

159

high-stakes private games are held most every night in more towns great and small than you could shake your dick at! Why not suggest a corporal's squad of lawmen guarding every bank and a Cavalry troop, with their horses, aboard every train. It's a matter of simple economics, old son. The powers-that-be would rather chance a few robberies than pay the cost of total prevention. We were talking before about the crooks having the edge on initiative."

Longarm insisted, "Back up and hear me out. I know we can't stake out all the games of chance in this land of opportunity. I'm talking about a baited trap. A high-stakes game to write home about and ask them to send you money. I figure our Great Garrick's overdue for another strike. So he's holding off for a bigger score as this fall's beef sales are in full swing, with a heap of ready cash to be won or lost at the turn of a card and—"

"Where?" Billy Vail cut in, exploding a cloud of stinky smoke so that only his voice gave his presence away as it pontificated, "It ain't like we were back in the days of the long cattle drives out of cow-crowded Texas to the few railroad towns to the north. Thanks to Flying Time and American Enterprise, they got trains in Texas and they're raising cows as far north as the for Gawd's sake Peace River Range in Canada! So the Eastern buyers with ready cash will be dickering with cattle barons all over the West most anytime now. Nobody has to drive cows to just the few railroad terminals they used to. Texas being left behind the door when the rails were being laid during the war and Reconstruction, some Texas beef is still being trailed north, to where the owners figure on getting the best price, and that varies a heap from year to year."

As his features slowly emerged from the fog, Vail's lips were moving as he silently counted. Then he shook his bullet head and said, "I was right the first time I thought of a setup. There's just too many good-sized cow towns these days to be worth such expensive stabs in the dark. Even if you could convince all the high rollers in town you were holding such a wondrous opportunity, how could we even hope our bad actor was anywheres near that particular town? So far, he's struck all over the country, only *mostly* in the West because there's so much more country out our way. What if you set and baited your trap in Dodge or Cheyenne whilst he was hand-loading them two Le Mats in Frisco or, shit, right here in Denver?"

Longarm brightened and said, "Wouldn't cost as much to establish such a game here in Denver. I could ask some reporter pals on the *Post* or *News* to plant gossip about a convention of high rollers having Denver PD on the prod. I could ask my pal Sergeant Nolan to alert some roundsmen to watch out for trouble with such high stakes on their beat, and Lord knows we have our own notorious gamblers to invite. Rowdy Joe Lowe and his sort of rowdy Kate are living quieter, right here in Denver, after Rowdy Joe came so close to getting hung in Texas. Then there's Corn Hole Johnny, Chuck-a-Luck Johnny and Three-Card Johnny . . ."

"He ain't in Denver and all three of him's John Gallagher," Vail cut in, adding with a smug smirk, "You ought to pay more attention to our Henry's cross-indexing in the files."

He went on, "The high-rolling Jim Moon has retired to his native New York with his ill-gotten gains. Pony Reid is currently dealing faro out on the Barbary Coast, whilst Tricky Brown was last heard from in San Antone and I'll have your badge and your heart on a stick if you go inviting old Silver Dollar Tabor or Bet-a-Million Gates to serve as bait for a known killer!"

"Gates is in Chicago at the moment." Longarm shrugged. Then he flicked more ashes, sighed and said, "Whan you're right, you're right. Where do you set one

161

beaver trap when beavers are free to splash in any creek in a whole lot of country? Can I go grab something to eat now? My guts are growling fit to bust."

Vail glanced at the banjo clock on one oak-paneled wall, and seeing a chance to reward a good lawman for a job well done without appearing a soft touch, he snarled, "Go on then. The afternoon's about shot. But see you only indulge in enough beer at the Parthenon to justify the free lunch, and write me that full report before you bed down for the night just down Sherman Street from us. My wife says the two of you ought to be ashamed of yourselves."

As Longarm rose he was able to assure his boss with a straight face that his wife had nothing to worry about up on Capitol Hill that evening. (He felt no call to say he meant to shack up on Lincoln Street with another of his regular pals.) Rich widows on Sherman with their own opera boxes were to be avoided with the fall opera season coming on.

He left, as Billy Vail had predicted, for the nearby lavish Parthenon Saloon, where they overcharged for drinks but set a fine spread of cold cuts, three kinds of cheese, devilish eggs and such, along with fresh-baked bread from that big bakery owned and operated by full-blooded but wised-up Arapaho.

As he was building himself a heroic sandwich, Longarm spotted a face in the crowd and elbowed his way through the same with the sandwich in one hand and a schooner of needled beer in the other.

Reporter Crawford of the *Denver Post* started out broader across the beam than Longarm, but after that he wasn't as experienced at working his way to the bar through a crowd.

Longarm was just as glad to catch Crawford thirsty.

He said, "You may be just the man I want to see. I heard Rowdy Joe Lowe and Rowdy Kate were running a card house here in Denver. Nobody around the federal building could tell me where. Your turn."

The reporter, who was paid to be nosy, said, "I'm not certain his common-law wife's still with him. He's not running card games these days. He's providing she-male companionship for visitors to the Mile High City, over near the stockyards."

Longarm whistled and marveled, "Rowdy Joe Lowe's been reduced to pimping in his declining years?"

Crawford replied, "I just said that. Don't decline if you want to live high on the hog. I don't know which is more insufferable, a famous beauty or a notorious gunfighter, but neither gets to flap their wings and crow at the sun to come up for them that many sunrises. Can we carry this over to the bar? I never came in here to recite the sad tale of Rowdy Joe Lowe."

Longarm turned his back to the current to move slow and sure as an icebreaker, with the reporter following in his wake, saying, "It was, let's see, going on ten years since he shot it out in Newton with a gun slick, buried under the name of *Sweet*, over Rowdy Kate. *She* was ten years younger then, as well. It was eight or nine years back he had his famous shoot-out with E. T. Beard, known as Red Beard for natural reasons. Joe tried to plead it had been self-defense, but the coroner's jury had a hard time buying that the shotgun Rowdy Joe had carried in to Beard's saloon was for a friendly business discussion. So Rowdy Joe jumped bail and lit out for Texas, where he had a few tense discussions in Dennison, Fort Worth and Waco without anybody ever proving anyone had died."

As Longarm got them to the bar, the reporter said, "I wasn't there; I don't know what happened. Maybe it was one close call too many. Maybe it was a lot of close calls spread out across a lot of years and then Rowdy Joe was neither as young nor as rowdy as he'd been in, say, Ellsworth in the first flush of the postwar cattle boom. As I said, I don't know if his no-longer-young Rowdy Kate is still with him. I understand he lives in a boardinghouse over on Blake Street. Don't have the exact address. He mostly pimps in the saloons near the stock and railroad yards. Why do you want to scout him up? He's old news, unless you're holding out on a pal!"

Longarm shook his head and said, "I just wanted a professional advising me on tricks of his trade. How you'd word a personal invite to a sporting gent without scaring or insulting him. How you'd go about making up such a guest list. Stuff like that. Whether he's lost his nerve or just grown up, Rowdy Joe may have put on the sort of show I'm interested in. See if you can belly to the bar as I sort of rotate my ass away from the same."

Crawford could. Longarm took some time getting out the distant doors to the street, and by then he'd washed his sandwich down and set the now-empty schooner on a sill, handy to the way out.

Once outside he saw that the summer sun was low and squinty in the northwest. They'd laid out downtown Denver's numbered streets northwest to southeast. So the cross streets with names were now shaded from side to side, and he had to trudge down 17th Street with the sun right in his eyes.

Longarm lowered his hat brim to where he could navigate less painfully while staring down at the sun-dazzled sandstone walk. As he strode towards the rail and stock yards, he rehearsed how he meant to ask a washed-up gambler how to help him trap someone likely more up-to-date about such doings.

The more he went over what they had on their yellow sheets about the erstwhile terror of cow-town card houses, the more Longarm wondered if he might be wasting time. He didn't recall anything about Rowdy Joe staging games more private than he'd staged in the back rooms of saloons he and Rowdy Kate had run.

After almost walking into the wheels of a beer dray on Curtis Street when he got as far as Arapahoe and 17th, he paid more mind to the tricky light, as he saw that the rush hour had commenced. The saloons ahead would be loaded with strange faces as he canvassed them for a middle-aged pimp who might or might not be on the streets that evening.

As Longarm got to the wider and busier Larimer Street, he reined in to wait for a break in the traffic. As he stood there he recalled how he'd planned to head on home to his furnished digs to shit, shave, shower and shine for his more serious interview up on Lincoln. Seeing he'd be in the shade along Larimer as he headed for the bridge across Cherry Creek, Longarm decided, "Hell with Rowdy Joe!" as he turned on one heel to cut southeast instead of northwest as expected.

So when two horse pistols roared as one, they sent a fusillade of hot lead through the break in the traffic. Longarm headed for the cover of a brick building on the corner of 17th and Larimer way faster than he usually walked, with his would-be assassin adjusting range and windage to pluck at his coattails with fingers of sudden death.

Chapter 19

A draft horse hit in the rump with birdshot can cause considerable confusion as it bolts through heavy traffic, with the bread wagon it's bolted to scattering loaves right and left as it tilts from side to side a ways before crashing total.

Meanwhile, Longarm had drawn his .44-40 and dropped to the walk around the corner to lizard on his vest buttons whilst he took off his hat to risk a peek around the bricks at ground level.

As he'd feared, the southeast-to-northwest 17th Street he'd had to leave so sudden was filled clean across with sun-dazzled, cotton white gunsmoke. Longarm legged it across to move southeast along the far side of 17th in the unlikely event his noisy admirer was laying for him on the crowded streets of Denver during a rush hour.

The smoke was thinning by the time he made it to about the point from which it had all billowed forth. By then Longarm had his badge pinned to his tweed lapel to explain the six-gun in his hand. As he crossed over, he met a blue-uniformed copper badge who'd responded to the sounds of gunfire. They had met before. When Denver PD asked who'd been shooting at whom, Longarm said,

"I was the intended target; we're still working on the who. That's likely why he, she or it just tried to back-shoot me if I'm right about the weapons. If I've guessed right, I must be getting warm!"

He'd guessed right, they determined within minutes by digging a few spent rounds of .41-caliber slugs with casting seams out of that one wrecked bread wagon.

By then the peppered draft horse and with two others injured in the melee had been carried off to be treated by their vets. Birdshot looked like birdshot no matter what it was shot from, and buckshot would have lamed the draft horse worse.

Other copper badges, Crawford of the *Post* and Reporter Page of the *Rocky Mountain News* were now on the scene. Denver PD canvassing 17th Street had come up with two witnesses who agreed the shootist had been a Papist nun, or a convincing imitation of one, who'd popped out of a doorway to throw down on Longarm with a big horse pistol in each hand, filling the street with gunsmoke and vanishing in the same. One of the roundsmen found a nun's habit in a hallway that ran clean through a layout with shops at street level and tenement flats above. Canvassing the folk who lived over the shops only established that the hallway led clean back to the alley, and that nobody had seen nothing in the alley.

So, having better ways to spend an evening than to chase his own tail in circles, Longarm told the local law and newspapermen the simple truth, offered no suggestions as to who might have wanted to gun down a federal deputy on his way home, then went somewhere else to shit, shave, shower and shine for his date with more pleasant company on Lincoln Street.

He didn't tell her about the close call at 17th and Larimer. When you told gals about close calls it gave them the excuse to bring up that safe job for more pay they all seemed to know about.

The next day, back at the office, Billy Vail was sort of war-dancing around his desk, waving his stinky cigar like a smouldering tomahawk as he pissed and moaned, "You wild and crazy asshole! Where did you go after that other maniac tried to clean your plow with a brace of Le Mats? I had the boys out searching for you high, low and sideways! How come you never reported back to me when you had such a close call?"

Longarm sat down to calmly reply, "I figured if you and the boys didn't know where I was, the Great Garrick wouldn't know where I was spending the night, and I had no call to pester you at home about things you couldn't do anything about. The sneaky shit got away clean. Or so he thinks. The nun's habit he was using as a disguise tells us he's a she, or a mighty short he."

"Unless he was bending at the knees," said a grimacing Vail, adding in a more cheerful tone, "The biggest mistake he made was letting us know he was here in Denver. I take back everything I said last night about him being anywheres in the country. This could be just the shithouse break we've been hoping for. The question before the house now is whether he's in town to rob another private game or murder you."

Longarm said, "Ain't no big games being held by invite-only here in town this week. He likely wants me out of the picture before he pulls his next big one, as I keep saying, during the fall beef sales."

Vail said, "If so, you must be getting warm. But I thought you just told me you had no idea who the Great Garrick could be!"

Longarm shrugged and asked, "Ain't a guilty conscience grand? Somewhere, sometime, somehow, I've spooked the son of a bitch into suspecting I know something. Before you ask, if I did I'd go arrest the son of a bitch."

Vail responded, "Your ease in cracking that copycat

case down in Santa Fe may have shook him up. Those malicious Mexicans went about things in a different way, but they were pretty slick, and you made them look like bush league beginners."

He sat down and added, "Whatever he's afraid you know, he knows you'll be leading the hunt for his ass now, and at the risk of turning your little head, you do have a rep for cutting sign. So what if he's out to kill you here in Denver and rob somebody else somewhere else?"

Longarm nodded and said, "That's more than likely. But since we know he's waiting in the wings to stage his murder mystery here in Denver, I'd say that gives us the golden opportunity to set and bait the trap you told me I couldn't."

Vail started to say he still couldn't. Then he glared through his blue tobacco smoke to growl, "Tell me about it."

So Longarm did, making hasty changes when the older lawman pointed out minor flaws in an overall plan Vail just couldn't shoot down entirely.

In the end, selling Billy Vail on as good a shot as they were likely to get proved easier than selling it to some few others who just had to know what was going on if the plan was to have an outside chance.

First things coming first, Longarm let the excitement at 17th and Larimer die on the back pages whilst he took the natural steps of a lawman on the prod after someone tried to back-shoot him. He let it be known, whilst sitting with his back to the wall on those rare occasions he appeared in public, that he suspected that one of any number of old boys he'd put away in his six or eight years toting a badge was trying to make good on one of those threats lawmen got all the time.

Playing tag with the killer, if the killer was still in town, Longarm let other news leak out as if it had nothing to do with him or any other federal lawman.

Getting Reporter Crawford to plant the story took some arm-twisting. The portly reporter was inclined to buckskin up anything with a Wild West odor, but insisted that unlike some he never outright lied. When Reporter Crawford said there'd been a shoot-out he meant there'd been a shoot-out, even when nobody dead or alive had been anything more buckskin than a ribbon clerk or house painter. So when Longarm told Crawford what he wanted, the reporter shook his derby and said, "I don't like it. You're asking me to make up notorious high rollers who've never rolled and invite them to this private game across from the Union Station that's not fixing to take place and the *Denver Post* is a *news*paper, damn it!"

Longarm said, "You ain't been listening, and I've offered you a scoop on a silver platter, pard! I never asked you to make up notorious shit; I've already invented them for you. You only have to convince your readers they may be in town, for openers. That ain't an outright lie when you study on it. For who can say who may or may not be in town?"

Crawford laughed and said, "That's sophistry and we both know it. Even if I just run unsubstantiated rumors about something big coming up in high-rolling circles, how do invited guests who don't exist show up for private game that isn't going to occur?"

Longarm snorted, "How could the famous Saratoga Red host a private game in a secret location if you printed the address in your infernal paper? I mean to let the sneaky bastard *work* some before he figures out where we're playing with hundred-dollar chips behind a locked door."

The reporter frowned and asked, "Who's Saratoga Red? How come I've never heard of him if he's so famous?"

Longarm joshed, "Sure you've heard of him, old son.

170

Don't you remember the time I cut the cards with Bet-a-Million Gates for double or nothing?"

Crawford protested, "You can't ask me to run that. The real Bet-a-Million Gates would demand a retraction, and my city desk would surely ask me why!"

Longarm soothed, "Bet-a-Million will be pleased as punch by my brag if I let him lose. He don't really bet to win or lose. He sells barbed wire and bullshit. Stories about him being such a good loser are meant to make him famous to prospective customers. He don't care what you print about him as long as you spell his name right. Silver Dollar Tabor never asks for retractions, neither. He likes to see his name in print. So, come to study on it, don't you remember that time Saratoga Red was dealing when old Silver Dollar lost that considerable sum to Poker Alice, and paid off like a sport?"

"Poker Alice Ivers is a fake as well?" marveled the reporter.

Longarm said, "Nope, but she's a pal of mine and it'll be all right. You surely know how to sell a famous ganbler to your readers, damn it. Didn't you go along with the invention of Calamity Jane? Convincing just one of your readers the notorious Saratoga Red's in town to hold one of his notorious private games by invitation only might put an end to these mass murders, old hoss!"

So Reporter Crawford went along with the plan by planting murky gossip and an interview with a certain police lieutenant about the well-known but far from welcome Saratoga Red planning something big in Denver. Once he got his back into it, Reporter Crawford had the sporting crowd in Denver all abuzz over a famous high roller they naturally knew, personally.

Having studied the art of stage makeup traveling with the Divine Sarah's French Variety Company as well as Archer Bannerman's bunch more recently, Longarm decided he'd have the whiskers and haircut of Buffalo Bill, in brick red, albeit under an opera hat such as Luke Short and other Eastern sporting gents wore.

Made up to look more like his mother's side, Deputy Smiley allowed he'd be proud to guard the door as Fort Smith Fred, a heap bad member of the Five Civilized Tribes. Other deputies with less distinctive features got a kick out of the wigs, fake beards and flashy duds Longarm gathered up with the help of his plump drama coach out to the university, and if he had to kiss her, French, it made certain nobody along Larimer would gossip about a run on theatrical supplies.

They waited, and then one night, well after dark, Saratoga Red and the sinister Fort Smith Fred got to the Burlington Hotel across from the Union Station to set things up. Longarm warned Smiley not to look at him that way, as if he'd never seen a redheaded gent in a top hat before, as they were going in. So Smiley managed to wear the expression of a cigar store relative as Longarm laid things out for the night clerk and hotel staff before they went on up with their four overnight bags. He'd already established that none of the staff had been hired since Reporter Crawford had planted the first few seeds alongside the regular grapevine.

As they took over the corner suite on the top floor, Smiley sniffed and said somebody was brewing coffee down the hall. Longarm said, "That's not against any rules if you use one of those bitty alcohol cookers, but seeing others may be holed up close enough to overhear us, make sure we talk as if we're playing cards or, failing that, say 'rhubarb, rhubarb, rhubarb.' It's a trick I learned in my role as Reliable Steve. I'll 'splain it to you later. Just do it for now."

Smiley helped him set up the folding table and poker layout whilst he dryly muttered, "Rhubarb, rhubarb, rhubarb . . ."

After due time Deputy Macy arrived, looking ten years

older and a hundred times richer in his brocaded silk vest and broadcloth frock coat. As coached in advance, Macy loudly announced he was "loaded for bear and out to go home with all the money."

Deputy Dutch came in, dressed to the nines and reeking of a rich dude's cologne to declare his Leadville mining pal was full of shit and to promise he'd win his money, his watch and his woman, too.

And so it went until what appeared to be a quartet of high rollers was seated at the card table with Saratoga Red whilst Fort Smith Fred guarded the shut and barrel-bolted door. Having nothing better to say and seeing what they'd really paid for hundred-dollar chips, they proceeded to play poker, in the carefree manner of big shots who could afford to lose. It was way more fun to play poker when it didn't cost your own money when you lost. Anyone listening in, Longarm knew, would be likely to buy his bunch as high rollers with deep pockets indeed.

There came a tap on the door. Smiley glanced at Longarm, who nodded, his gun in his lap. Smiley opened up for the bitty old colored waiter from downstairs; Longarm remembered his name was Calvin, because he made a point of remembering the names of the often-overlooked.

Calvin asked in his fawning, humble darky way if he could fetch them any drinks from downstairs. Longarm, as Saratoga Red, told him they were serious sporting men with serious money at stake, so the six of them would be having coffee, unless anyone objected.

All the other high rollers allowed coffee was jake with them. Dutch was impish enough to ask for a shot of sherry with plenty of sugar in his mug.

The elderly colored man left and they played on for a spell, with Macy winning more than Dutch thought fair and Saratoga Red warning Dutch to be a sport. Then old Calvin came back with their coffee, accepted his tip with more bowing and scraping and let them go on with their charade.

So they did, sipping java and jawing idly as another hour passed and not a thing happened. As a distant clock struck ten, Fort Smith Fred turned from the door with an expression of disgust to say, "It's quiet as a tomb outside. How long do we have to keep this up?"

Longarm yawned and said, "Until something happens, of course."

It was Macy's deal. He seemed to be just sitting there with his eyes half shut. None of the others appeared to care. Dutch put his head down on the table and commenced to snore. Over by the door, Smiley had slid down the wall and then over on one side with his eyes shut.

Longarm muttered, "Aw, shit, I might have known," as he started to rise from the table, fell back in his chair and rolled out of it to lie half under the table with his six-gun drawn but gripped by the limp fingers of the dead or drugged.

After nobody had moved for a spell, the barrel bolt slid open as if by magic and old Calvin, or a mighty close resemblance, eased inside with a loaded Le Mat in each hand to kick the door shut behind him with a boot heel.

Surveying the room with the satisfaction of the true artist, the Great Garrick declaimed, "Your last performance was a total flop, Longarm! Did you really think you could fool an actor as great as I with greasepaint and hired hair? I knew all along what you were planning here in Denver, and you made it all so easy for me."

Moving across the rug with catlike stealth, the small white man with dark greasepaint and a woolly white wig smiled smugly and treated himself to, "Good night, Sweet Prince. I'd better finish *you* first."

Chapter 20

When a wild-eyed cuss in blackface is grinning down at you with a loaded and capped Le Mat in each hand, you shoot to kill.

So Longarm swung his six-gun up off the rug and shot to kill, again and again, until Whispers MacUlric wasn't standing there anymore.

Then he rolled across the rug three times and sprang to his feet in the smoke-filled room to move over to the window and fling it open wide before he went to the door and did the same, shedding his top hat, red beard and wig as he did so.

By the time the smoke had cleared enough to matter, Longarm had reloaded and pinned his badge to the front of his stage costume. He was admiring the black-thread stage magic MacUlric had rigged in advance to open the barrel bolt from outside when the real old Calvin appeared on the scene with two copper badges in blue.

Longarm introduced himself and said, "It's all over but for letting nature take its course. We set a trap for a mass murderer and he walked right into it, hugging himself for feeling so slick."

The smoke had cleared by then to where they could

see all the bodies stretched out on the rug. One of the roundsmen gasped, "Jesus, Mary and Joseph! How many lie dead?"

Longarm said, "Just one. The others will be coming around in a minute or more. They've been drugged with chloral hydrate, the knockout drops of choice in many a whorehouse. It's preferred beyond most others because it's seldom fatal and has no taste and hardly any smell."

He moved over to where Deputy Smiley sprawled, bent over for a better look and added, "It was lucky for me just now that chloral hydrate does have *some* smell and that once you've survived a whiff, you never forget it."

Calvin caught sight of the Great Garrick, oozing blood from many a bullet hole, and demanded, "Who that colored boy in hotel livery? Ain't nobody like that working at this hotel!"

Longarm was too polite to say that one elderly darky in the same uniform could be confused with a damned good makeup job by gaslight when you didn't know either all that well. Instead, he explained, "He's not a colored man. I'm sure he checked in earlier as a nondescript white man, on this floor if not next door. We smelled the coffee he had ready to serve in his room when we first got here."

Calvin said, "Oh, that would be Mister Davidson in the suite next door. He did say he liked to brew his own coffee on his own alcohol heater."

Longarm moved over to where MacUlric sprawled, muttering, "David's son, as in David Garrick. Billy Vail was supposed to figure that out as he and the rest of the boys cleaned up this mess. I wonder what it feels like to be certain you're smarter than everyone else in this world."

Then he decided he didn't want to know. There were some feelings, such as being scared of spiders or wanting to fuck sheep, it was likely just as well you never felt.

The deputy called Dutch because nobody could pronounce his old-country name was tough as they came, and he'd diluted his chloral hydrate by adding sugar to the sherry MacUlric had laced his drugged coffee with.

So he was first to stir, suddenly whipping out his six-gun to sit bolt upright and demand, "What's going on here? When did all these others get here? What am I doing with piss in my pants?"

Longarm said, "You were served knockout drops in your coffee. That gentleman of color near the doorway never came by to take our order. We never rang for room service with that pull cord near the door. That other gentleman of color, on the floor yonder, checked in just next door as a white man, turned himself into a reasonable facsimile and came by to take our orders. Then instead of going down to the kitchen, he prepared a tray in the very next room, drugged every cup with knockout drops and figured he only had to wait until we were all knocked out before he laid us all out around the table, artistical, to finish us off with a fusillade from those two big horse pistols you see to either side of him."

Deputy Macy was sitting up, shaking his head like it was full of water, as Dutch marveled, "Who was he? What was he? Some sort of stage magician?"

Longarm said, "He may have picked some up in his travels, working backstage for many a year. But he was what they call a prompter; he said he was a playwright as well. His name was MacUlric. He was with that acting company I spent some time with up in Fort Collins. I knew as soon as he tried to kill me here in Denver it had to be him, a stage manager named Froggy or a scenery shifter and understudy called Will Penny. I'm just as glad it was Whispers MacUlric—I liked Froggy and Will better."

"How come?" asked Dutch, adding, "Not how come

177

you liked others better than this shit. How come you could narrow it down so tight?"

Longarm said, "Old Billy's process of eliminating. When I saw that the gun that tried to eliminate me on the corner of 17th and Larimer had been a Le Mat, I eliminate pals of The Eel. So who did that leave?"

He holstered his .44-40 and fished out a smoke as he said, "Witnesses said the shootist had been short enough to pass for a nun. Had to be a man, because gals don't tote such man-sized guns. So how many short suspects had I been close enough to for them to feel so threatened as I blundered through their neck of the woods? My cracking that copycat case in Santa Fe presented no threat to the real deal and I'd hardly met up with anybody else since I caught other crooks entire!"

He lit his smoke and continued. "My checking into the same hotel as MacUlric up in Fort Collins was the sheer shithouse break Billy *told* me we needed. The odds of a lawman joining up with MacUlric's theatrical company under an assumed name must have struck his worried mind as a shit-in-your-britches cat-and-mouse game when I told him and the others who I really was. He knew he'd told me right out he was planning to start his own touring company, on a prompter's wages, and that he'd be in Omaha come the fall beef sales!"

From where he lounged on the floor, Smiley said, "He figured you were on to him, couldn't prove it and figured to pounce up Omaha way!"

Dutch declared, "I see it all now. He figured to eliminate you first!"

Longarm blew smoke out his nostrils, nodded and continued. "Like our old Billy likes to say, a guilty conscience can lead a crook to jump with both feet into quicksand conclusions. I'd forgot all about the Bannerman company until their prompter emptied a brace of Le Mats in my direction here in Denver. Once I'd eliminated other

178

Fort Collins suspects because they wouldn't add up as our touring mass murderer, I added what MacUlric and others had said about being in Omaha this fall, saw I had no way on earth of guessing where he'd strike up yonder and set out to stop him here."

From where he still sprawled on the floot, the lanky Deputy Smiley asked in a matter-of-fact tone, "How come that dead fool in blackface didn't just leave sleeping dogs lie? You'd left Fort Collins without suspecting shit. He could have just given Omaha a pass and robbed another private card game later, somewhere else."

Longarm nodded but said, "He fancied himself a great playwright as well as a great actor. It must have galled him to watch from the footlights, night after night, as sincerely bad actors put on an awesomely bad temperance play. Whispers told me, before he knew who I was, he'd soon be in the market for a juvenile lead with stage presence."

He blew a modest smoke ring and explained, "That's actor talk for a hero who can sort of take over a scene in a play."

Dutch snorted, "Oh, save me! Save me! You big brave man!"

Longarm laughed and said, "I know it all sounds dumb. But his guilty conscience drove him dumber. I've yet to determine what sort of excuse Whispers gave Archer Bannerman, but he must have given him one, and it's less than three hours by rail. So his guilty conscience was another shithouse break Billy Vail kept saying we'd need to catch him, and we did, and now somebody had best report all this to the coroner's office."

One of the copper badges said he was on his way. By the time he returned with a grumpy-looking old cuss and two litter bearers, the rug around the late Whispers MacUlric was a hell of a mess and all the drugged deputies were recovering from his attempt to murder them.

By midnight they had MacUlric on ice at the county morgue and Billy Vail had joined them in the saloon across the way. So Longarm got to tell the whole tale over, and Billy wasn't satisfied.

He told Longarm, "Anyone can see MacUlric was out to kill you and the boys this evening. But how do we know he was working alone? How can we be sure you're not just guessing a lot of the details?"

Longarm said, "Eliminating. He was sort of a loner up in Fort Collins. Seemed to get along with the others, but when he wasn't prompting anybody he sort of looked through them, like he had more important things on his mind, and I reckon he did."

Vail said, "Not good enough. I want a report in depth, lest the newspapers catch me with my fly unbuttoned. This figures to run as front-page news in bold type, coast to coast. They're fixing to ask me where and when such a brooding genius—I can see the headlines now—might have gone wrong. I have to be able to give them more details on all his earlier killings across the country. I have to be able to tell them . . . Damn it, old son. You know what I need. Get up to Fort Collins and bring it back for me, damn it!"

So Longarm did. The first thing he found out was that Esperanza had up and quit, to appear in a more sensible play in Saint Lou. The distraught Archer Bannerman was too distraught to talk to anybody who didn't want to play Fair Violet. But Longarm soon learned Whispers had laid on some tripe about negotiating rights to his own great play out of town, more than once. He got that out of Froggy Hummel, Will Penny and the not-bad-looking actress who played Mother Dearest in a white wig; she wasn't that old offstage.

So within the day Longarm had all the vital statistics on the late Great Garrick, or two-faced Whispers Mac-Ulric, and since Froggy seemed to have the inside track with Mother Dearest, Longarm hopped a train back to Denver to get in around sundown.

He knew Billy Vail didn't want to see him again before he'd written his officious report, and meanwhile he'd promised old Cloressa Chandler, out by the university, he'd return the borrowed properties and give her an oral account of how things turned out.

So he bundled all the costumes, beards and wigs in a laundry bag, threw it over his shoulder and hopped the Broadway Line out to South Denver.

A little kid riding the streetcar with his pretty mother or an older sister asked Longarm if he was Santa Claus. His pretty mother or older sister cuffed his ear and told him not to sass his elders.

Longarm soberly assured the kid he was only an elf.

Out at the private quarters of the not exactly homely but more than pleasantly plump Cloressa, he was greeted by a worried hug as his drama coach gasped, "Oh, Custis, I was so worried about you! And that was even before I read about that horrid monster slipping you knockout drops!"

She hugged considerable because there was so much of her, clad at the moment in a black velvet kimono that made a man feel sort of dirty no matter where he hugged her back.

As he picked up the bag of stage items and she led him inside, Longarm explained, "That was how he got the drop on all those others, time after time. Being a fair character actor and quite a makeup artist, Whispers MacUlric was often able to just substitute himself for hotel help, as he almost managed to the other night. On those occasions that the real help showed up at the wrong time or just wouldn't get out of his way, MacUlric killed them, too, adding to the mystery by blurring the pattern some."

She told him to just set the bag at one end of her chesterfield and sat him down on the same. She took his hat and coat as he told her how the sneaky little shit had knocked out armed men who could have busted him over a knee to finish them off in one fusillade from those man-sized Le Mat horse pistols. She asked him if he might not feel more comfortable if he took his gun belt off.

He unbuckled the rig and set it aside on the tufted leather chesterfield whilst she served wine and cheese off the low-slung table in front of the same. He was sort of surprised to find the situation didn't scare him as much as he'd feared it might. If old Clo wasn't half as slender as Mother Dearest up Fort Collins way, she was way younger and, as a matter of fact, might have passed for pretty had she weighed a tad less.

Say a hundred pounds or so.

He could smell the fancy French perfume she's slathered over her bare flesh under that velvet kimono as he told her how he'd detected the chloral hydrate he'd suspected to begin with. He said, "I knew there was no way to just blaze away across a card table, time after time, and never catch any return fire. They tell a tale of a night in Dodge at the Long Branch Saloon where this one old boy called Levi Richardson, a buffalo hunter said to be a crack shot, shot a gambler called Frank Loving point blank and wound up dead on the floor when Loving got his own gun out and fired back."

As Clo leaned closer, he said, "That was one-on-one. Consider the odds of dropping half a dozen without a round of return fire, and you can see how I eliminated anything like a shoot-out."

Clo kissed him. He had to kiss her back, and once they got started he was just as glad Froggy had the inside track with Mother Dearest, and it sure beat all how riding down from Fort Collins with a hard-on for an older gal could slenderize perfumed flesh under feel-up velvet. So he tried to explain how Whispers MacUlric, frustrated as a great actor on stage and needing money to start his own the-

182

atrical company, had parlayed his bitter feelings towards taller and richer men into a series of what he'd planned as perfect crimes, "Likely enjoying the way he had us all fooled as much as he enjoyed his ill-gotten gains."

But she didn't seem to be interested, and once a gal had you unbuttoned to play French tunes on your old organ grinder it seemed only Christian to spread her out on the rug and treat her like a lady.

It didn't hurt a bit, and if you kept your eyes shut it was easier to think of such an opportunity as rising to a challenge rather than beastiality with a beached whale, and either way, it wasn't bad.

So Longarm got to the office later than usual with the handwritten report for Henry to type up. He had to present it to Billy Vail first, of course. As he did so, Billy shot him a knowing look and said, "I take it you caught a morning train down from Fort Collins after a pleasant roll in the feathers with that Fair Violet you kept saving from a fate worse than death?"

Longarm soberly replied, "There ain't no fate worse than death, and you have my word I never spent the night in Fort Collins with anybody."

So, knowing Longarm hardly ever lied outright, Billy Vail apologized for having such a dirty mind and they said no more about it.

Watch for

LONGARM AND THE DEVIL'S BRIDE

the 311th novel in the exciting LONGARM
series from Jove

Coming in October!

LONGARM

**Explore the exciting Old West with one
of the men who made it wild!**

J. R. ROBERTS

THE GUNSMITH